LAURA'S LEGACY

Laura Pennington is the wilful daughter of self-made man Obadiah Pennington. Having risen from being a humble fisherman's daughter, she is still adjusting to her new position in society. Then fate crosses her path in the person of Mr Daniel Tranton, who catches her trespassing on private land. Together they come to the aid of a young lad who has run away from servitude at a local mill. Neither realises that the men hunting him are also set on hurting Daniel. The future depends on Laura's quick thinking and actions . . .

VALERIE HOLMES

LAURA'S LEGACY

Complete and Unabridged

LINFORD
Leicester

First published in Great Britain

First Linford Edition
published 2016

A catalogue record for this book is available from the British Library.

ISBN 978–1–4448–2875–7

Published by
F. A. Thorpe (Publishing)
Anstey, Leicestershire

Set by Words & Graphics Ltd.
Anstey, Leicestershire
Printed and bound in Great Britain by
T. J. International Ltd., Padstow, Cornwall

This book is printed on acid-free paper

Prologue

Mr Obadiah Pennington's heart filled with pride as he walked over to his row of fishing boats. He glanced up at the line of terraces on the opposite cliff. He had done well for himself, but somehow the ale still tasted better in his old drinking hole, the Coble Inn, in the village.

A figure caught his attention, and his happiness was instantly cloaked by a veil of annoyance. Laura, his only child, was walking briskly across the gardens behind the old town of Ebton. He sighed. Her mother, for once, was quite right: she had no sense of how to behave. She was now old enough to wed; and, with his wealth and position in the town, she could marry well into new money.

Obadiah had been wondering how he was going to broach the subject of marriage to her, but now he knew the time to mention it had to be near at hand. There would be no flighty romances with the local fishermen for her. Instead, she would be matched to someone who was already established — or, at the very least, had good prospects.

He had two mill owners from the Tranton family in mind. This small coastal town was not a place for her. Both men were single, successful, and their cotton mills were within thirty miles of her home. He preferred the younger Tranton, Daniel. He'd been quite a lad in his younger days, but he was a fair man, and Obadiah respected him. Mrs Pennington wanted to approach his elder cousin, Mr Roderick Tranton, as his mill was nearer to them, being situated on the outskirts of Gorebeck only six miles inland. But Obadiah would not see her wed to a cold-hearted man. So he had written to the younger bachelor asking him to consider settling down with his beautiful, wilful daughter Laura. He prayed that the man would take the proposition seriously. Either way, as he watched her make for the pathway on the private land on the opposite side of the beck, he knew she was headed for the Hambleton estates, a place she had been forbidden to go.

'Obadiah!' The call from a fisherman approaching his boat meant he had to walk away, so Laura would have her way today — for the very last time. The next letter he hoped to receive would be one of introduction to Mr Daniel Tranton, making the first step in what he hoped would be a successful and contented union.

1

Laura woke and went to gaze out of her window, which overlooked the sweeping bay. The boats were already out and the seagulls flew around noisily, making their distinctive 'kwaarking' sound as they dived over the roofs and cliffs. They, too, were beginning a busy day.

She knew her father would already be out. He rose with the sun and did not want to lose a minute of the day — his favourite mantra was 'A minute lost is an opportunity thrown away!' She smiled. It was not one she totally shared, but her mother lost many opportunities as she did not rise before mid-day, now she was a lady of leisure, and then took an hour or so fussing with her maid about her outfit for the day — or what was left of it.

As Laura dressed herself, she set her sights on visiting the wooded gill, the private land beyond. It gave the best vantage point. The owners had erected fences and told the locals to stay off its grounds. Pathways they had used for many a year were now denied them. How, then, were they to challenge such highhandedness? Laura would. She had run along the west cliffs' path and down through the woodland to the beck as a child, and she had more status now as the daughter of a wealthy man — albeit one of trade, or many trades — than as just a local. So, with a defiant thought in her heart and happy memories of her wild childhood, she had quickly donned her most robust walking dress and decided to invade the neighbour's land. This act of bravery, as she saw it, was no less daring to her, with the knowledge that the gamekeeper and the master of the house were on a grouse hunt on Gorebeck Moor.

Laura skipped down the stairs and cut through the kitchens, grabbing a slab of parkin on her way. She stopped only long enough to drink some lemon juice, freshly made for her mama's waking, and then left through the back door. The servants, busy at their chores, hardly noticed as she slipped through the corridor between the laundry and the cold store. Only Mabel, the cook, saw her, and shook her head in a gesture of disgust. But Laura saw the smile on her lips and knew that she would not say a word against her.

Today, Laura would make a stand for the common man and woman, and walk the path of her childhood; or, at the very least, remember that thrill of excitement she had felt on such ventures as a child.

* * *

'Jeb Flitch! Jeb Flitch!' The voice bellowed from the mouth of the overseer of Gorebeck Cotton Mill.

'Where's Jeb?' a raggedy boy asked the one shuffling along next to him, the breath from his mouth dispersing as visible vapour on the air. They were answering the roll call, the start of another twelve-hour shift from before daylight broke till after the sun had set. The lad shrugged, digging his cold hands into the pockets of his old trousers, his downcast eyes staring at the ill-fitting boots that slipped as he rushed to be inside the factory doors before the bell finished ringing. The dew formed a slippery covering over the old cobblestones. Day was yet to dawn. He shrugged his shoulders; the answer was that nobody seemed to know. Jeb had vanished into the night.

'He's done a runner!' the formidable figure of Mrs Cookson bellowed as she came out of the school room. 'He should have been here an hour since, as punishment for falling asleep in me lessons yesterday evening, but instead he's up and gone.' She glared at the approaching boys as they passed by her room door and into the manufactory.

'He was hurt yesterday, Mrs Cookson,' the young girl, Esther, chirped up, but all it got her was a light slap on the back of her head from Mr Bullman, the overseer, for being insolent and speaking out of turn. They were only to answer when spoken to.

'Well, what if he was?' Mrs Cookson rounded on the girl, who now stood with watery eyes, pulling her tattered woollen shawl around her thin body. 'We all get hurt at times, but work is work and has to be done! You set them men of yours looking for him, Mr Bullman. They like a chase, and that little brat won't get far, not with his cuts and bruises.'

Mr Bullman waved the children onward into the mill. 'Aye, we'll catch him, and his will be a lesson you'll all remember. We provide a home here for you, and yet some of you are so lazy that you don't want to do an honest day's work to keep the mill going. Work hard today, and keep the silence as you think about the young fool Jeb Flitch. He's set his path, and it will not end happily . . . you can take my word upon that!'

* * *

Daniel rode into Gorebeck over the old drystone bridge. It still held the charm of a village, yet this North Yorkshire market town had grown so much since the days of his boyhood. The Norman church looked beautiful as he approached the bridge, but the new housing had all but replaced the cruck-built cottages that had once lined the muddy track leading to the market square.

He had received a most unusual letter from a man of means and a dubious past, who owned a good deal of coastal property in the bay of Ebton. Daniel knew Obadiah Pennington of old, from the days when he had been given his first horse and ridden around the area exploring it as if he owned it. His first encounters with Obadiah had brought him down a peg or two, but they had since traded between themselves and enjoyed, he reasoned, a mutual respect.

Apparently, Daniel had more of the man's trust than he had realised, as his only daughter had been offered up along with a portion of his trading routes to Holland and France. This was an interesting option, but for one slight problem: Daniel had no wish to marry. How to decline the girl without either offending her father or risking the trade, which he relied on for his mill, going to a competitor? He smiled as he thought of Roderick, his cousin, being one such possibility, but then his smile faded as he realised this might be an option Obadiah would consider.

He crossed the river, then his attention was taken by a commotion coming from a group of people gathering outside an alehouse. Five men poured out of the Hare and Rabbit Inn, led by a man he knew well . . . a very angry man.

'Mr Bullman, what is the trouble? Has something happened at the mill?' Daniel asked.

He could see the hunger in the group's eyes. It was not for food, as the community did quite well compared to the West Yorkshire mill towns, but it was the hunger for blood — the look of the chase.

'Aye, sir, Jeb Flitch has run, and you know Mr Roderick's view on that. Like in the Indies, runners need to be made to appreciate how good their fortune had been!'

'This is not the Indies, and those days are now behind us. Jeb is no more than a boy, if I remember him correctly, and . . .'

'Flitch is twelve summers if he is a day! He could have served in the wars. He is old enough to run like a man, and he is old enough to stand punishment for it.'

Daniel looked down at this group of men. Bullman's usual group of heavies. He would no doubt pay them with ale if they found the lad, terrified and hungry. If Daniel could ever place the blame for a crime at their door, he would break them before their power grew any further, but one major obstacle in disclosing them for the rabble they were was his cousin's belief that these returning soldiers were loyal to their country and the old ways. In Daniel's eyes, they were loyal only to themselves, and were perfect examples of Wellington's 'scum of the earth' who had returned true to type. These specimens had been fortunate enough to find work. He suspected they were bleeding Roderick dry, but could not prove it. If he could only talk to the man . . . but Roderick insisted that, as the elder, he was also the wiser one.

'How long has he been gone?' Daniel asked.

'Took off some time in the night. He'll be back before the day's out.' Bullman touched his tattered tall hat and waved his hand forward. 'Come on, lads. He's wounded prey; we'll be back drinking porter in no time.' They cheered, walked at a pace up the newly surfaced road, and headed out of the town.

Daniel had been on his way to see Roderick about how he ran his mill, and to discuss the meeting which was to be held on their doorstep by the mill workers in the area; but the words 'he's wounded prey' lingered in his mind. Jeb was a good lad: Daniel had seen him there many times. The lad loved horses, and had happily seen to Daniel's on his infrequent visits.

He dismounted and headed into the inn. Choosing to sit on the settle by the bay window, he ordered a drink, but waited for his chance to find out more about Bullman's latest source of entertainment. It soon came: young May had seen him enter, and her eyes were noticeably moist as she came over to see him.

'Victuals, sir?' she asked.

Daniel noticed how flushed her cheeks were, as if she were upset. Seeing this, he knew she could help him. 'They're hunting Jeb?'

She made to brush down the crumbs from the table with her cloth and nodded, barely able to hold the tears back.

'Help me, May, and I will find a way to help him. He is a good lad and I know you are fond of him.' May had been a child of the mill, but on her last birthday she had been offered work, and had left that life — for one not much better, but perhaps one that would give her the chance to find a husband.

'They're heading for the open moor, thinking he wants to hitch a ride to York or Whitby. You know, as if he would be thinking to lose himself in the port or city. But he won't, because he'd be too far off.' She glanced around to make sure that no one was overhearing her conversation.

'Then where?'

'To the sea, sir.' She sniffed. 'He's got a cut arm, though, and he might . . . It needs more help than I could give it, but he wants to go on the sea, and breathe fresh air.'

'Dreams, pipe dreams that could kill him. Thank you, May. I'll see if I can pick up his trail.'

'Sir, you won't bring him back, will you? I mean, Mr Roderick'll have him publicly beaten for this.'

'I give you my word that I will see him safe, and if he has a crime to answer for, it will be dealt with a kindly eye.' He finished his drink, stood, and left the tavern.

Later, approaching the moor road, his heart sank as he realised that May had been wrong. Bullman had also headed across the old monks' trods to the coast. They must have picked up the lad's trail. 'Damn!' he swore. He had made a promise, and even if it was to a wench that served in an alehouse, he would keep it.

2

Laura shielded her eyes with her bonnet as she looked at the view. Ebton had grown and changed so much since she was a small child. She watched the plume of smoke from one of the cottage's chimneys and remembered when, some fifteen years ago, one had gone up in flames. It was nestled behind the small Methodist chapel, and the whole village could have gone up in smoke had it not been for the quick-thinking inhabitants. Luckily, people had been up and about already. Having the German Ocean so near had helped their effort. Some said that they had been 'up and about' for no good lawful reason; but whatever that reason, that night they saved Ebton from burning down.

Laura's family had lived in one of the old fishermen's cottages near the beach back then. They were simple abodes, very different to the new stone houses on the opposite cliff where they lived now. People were literally able to look down on the old inn and town, but Laura had not made such a transition. She had loved her old home and its nearness to the elements, and the strong community that existed; but as time and progress had moved on, the community spirit had somehow weakened.

A famous gang of smugglers was broken up on the night of the fire, and the tales her grandpa had told her were captivating, fanning a desire within her for more in life than embroidery, chores and basic learning. She wanted to feel that same childhood excitement again. Not from the closeness of a fire, but to have her senses tingle so that she knew what it felt like to be truly alive. The danger was frightening, but surviving it meant knowing how wonderful it was to be safe with a lifetime before you. Perhaps it explained her restless nature; her tendency to take small risks, knowing they could have bigger consequences if she were discovered. Laura always told herself that she was a survivor; it was her father's legacy to her. He had survived the gangs, the unrest of a period in the villagers' lives when they all went to ground or died. He had seen his moment of opportunity and acted, and because of this the family thrived, as he was now a respectable businessman. Ebton was an example of respectability, as was he, and she wondered sometimes if he still craved for a time that was more challenging.

She smiled as she watched the fishing boats being brought up onto the beach, laden with their catch. One was preparing to leave. She could not tell who was on it, but it looked to be one of her father's. He would be furious with her if he knew where she was, but she smiled, for he was always too busy to care these days.

Laura loved her life, but she was forgetting herself, forgetting where she was, and that was dangerous. This was private land and she had no right to be on it, yet up here she could see the sea and wonder at its mesmerising beauty, and watch the activity upon it: a myriad of vessels making their way up and down the coast, from London to Newcastle and foreign lands far beyond. She breathed in, wondering what it would be like to set sail across the vast expanse of water, a dot on the edge of violent waves one moment and in the swell of a calm flowing ocean the next, beyond control at the will of nature. The whaling port of Whitby further south was larger, but their town was growing and changing — and Laura was, too. No longer a child, she was now a beautiful woman with soft curls of a light auburn hue. Ebton was becoming known, a town where people travelled to take the waters and bathe, to breathe the sea air; she loved it, and all the people that were appearing in this quite remote part of the coast.

Lost to her thoughts, she carelessly

tripped over a small branch. The basket she was carrying fell to the ground next to her. She swore to herself because now she had a mark on her skirts. Feeling like a naughty child again, she laughed; this was not the sort of excitement from her past that she had been thinking about.

She bent double to try and brush away the soil from the fabric without smudging it further, but fell to the ground as a pistol shot rang out above her head. It had come through the woodland. Quickly, Laura pulled herself up and stood straight, her basket discarded. She leaned back against the rough bark of an ash tree, listening intently for any noise to try and determine what was happening.

It had been foolish to enter the woodland on her own, she knew it, and then to stand around as if she owned the land and the view beyond. Laura had forgotten time; she had been in a daze watching, listening and enjoying the freedom. Yet she had been stupid enough to risk being caught. Why? Because she had wanted to pick the wild garlic whilst it was still fresh. It thrived on this side of the steep gill, and she could not see what harm it would do for her to collect some. Besides, she believed that the wild crops of the land were a gift of nature and should be shared. The owner never touched it. Or had she just decided to commit this rash act because she had been forbidden to roam here?

Laura flinched as another shot rang out, nearer this time. She let out a stifled scream as it splintered a branch on a tree opposite her. That was too close. She must either run for her life or risk being shot. The sense of danger she had craved was now only too near. Voices carried on the light breeze: 'That way — get him!'

A hunt was underway. Why were they chasing anything? The noises she was hearing were all human, not the bustling panic of a startled animal fleeing for its life.

'Over here!' another voice rang out, the accent not quite local. So who were they, and why were strangers scouring the land — surely not for her? No, of course not; they had said 'him'. She swallowed. Whoever he was, they were too close for her comfort and safety.

Laura grabbed her basket and ran for dear life. She was trespassing — these lands were not common ground; and, looking at the basket filled with the fruits of the forest and her lovely garlic, she realised that her desire and belief in her right to use nature's free gifts could be construed as theft.

Laura half-ran, half-slipped down a bank and tried to take a lower path that lined the edge of the beck that had carved out this ancient gill. The water was low, so she reasoned she could follow the actual course of the water to get back to the old town, and continue from there to the safety of her home. It was what the old smugglers in the region had done; and although it was very dangerous if there were a flash flood from the higher land that fed the stream, at least it offered a quick way back to Ebton and safety. She saw that today she could cross below the bend and then she would be off the estate lands.

Laura calmed her breathing. *Stay in control*, she thought. Her trembling subsided until she heard rustling in the ferns behind her, and then she panicked. Her feet touched the lower path and she slipped; her long skirt caught on the undergrowth, tugging at brambles and briars. She lost hold of her basket and sadly saw its contents flow back to nature. Laura watched helplessly as it floated away downstream; her favourite basket gone as well.

Another shot was fired, but this time it appeared to be over the land above her; not at her, though, as the noise was more distant. For a moment she stopped tugging and just lay still against the bank, her skirt pinning her there.

'Thank God!' she muttered as she regained her composure, and admonished herself for being so careless with the results of her morning's labour. She had risked her safety for nothing, and lost a basket that she had taken great pleasure in making herself. Old Amy from the inn had shown her how.

A noise above her made her grasp frantically at the skirt material, trying desperately to free it; but before she could turn, a man slid down the bank next to her. His hand grabbed hers as he descended. Roughly, he ripped the fabric free, bringing some undergrowth with it, but releasing her garment with only one small snag to show for the struggle.

Desperate to release herself from his grip, she pulled away as hard as she could, but he did not stop to introduce himself or explain his actions. Instead of breaking free, Laura found herself unwittingly running hand in hand with the dark-haired stranger. He crossed the gill to the opposite bank and, without pausing, pulled her up the other side to the path hidden by ancient oak and ash trees. The crack of a distant shot told her that her pursuers had moved further down the woods on the far side and had lost their trail. She stared up at the stranger's face to see an unmistakable look of relief upon it. Then he smiled at her as she stared blankly at him, wondering who or what he was.

Laura tugged her hand from his. She knew a place behind a large boulder, overgrown by ivy, where she would be hidden from view if she could only break away from him, but not if he watched her slip into it. Desperation and frustration grew as she looked at the man directly; he was in his prime, fine of feature, and was looking straight back into her eyes in a direct way.

'Who are you, sir?' she snapped out the words.

'You must come with me.' Ignoring her efforts to pull away, as if she had the futile strength of a child, he held her hand firmly, turned, and half-walked, half-dragged her up the path along the gill away from her home.

'Let me go or I will scream and shout and have the villagers fall upon you, sir!' Laura protested.

'That you will not!' he said back to her as he glanced over his shoulder. His confidence irritated her.

'I will!' Now she felt like a child, expecting him to chant 'Will not!' in response.

He stopped and stared at her as if searching her very soul. 'No, you will not, because you were running too; and that means you were up to no good, or trespassing. So be silent and come with me without further fuss. I will explain once we are there.'

'Why should I? Where's there?' Laura demanded as she stumbled along behind him, still being led by her hand like an unruly child.

'Because I have asked you to, and I need your help.' He did not slow his pace.

'You have not asked me at all!' Laura's voice rose.

He spun around, sighed, and through

dark brown eyes that were looking at her imploringly, changed his tone and softened his words. 'Miss, please help me. I have a friend who could be dying as we speak. I need your help.' He tilted his head and his eyes studied her curiously.

'Very well, show me this friend of yours, and then you can explain all quickly, whilst I decide what is to be done,' Laura responded, without thinking of the stupidity of her words.

He nodded, oblivious to her troubled thoughts and seemingly ignoring her declarations of what she would or would not do. Yet still he held on to her as he branched off the path and headed directly for her hidden place behind the large overgrown boulder.

3

'He's in here,' the stranger said, moving the undergrowth aside.

Laura froze, angry that her childhood hiding place had been so easily discovered. 'I will not enter there with you! Who is he, anyway?'

'We need your help; and, seeing as you are running from them too, I would say that you are the one who has been placed in our path to provide it.'

A lock of dark hair fell across his cheek as he paused and waited for her to move forward. It was not exactly anger that Laura read into his expression, but what she would describe as impatience. She had no intention of slipping into a dark cavern with two 'outlaws' — he must think she was a dimwit or a completely immoral woman.

'No one placed me in your path! And it was you who was running, not I,' she added, tilting her head upwards in defiance as she tried to take a step back. But he held her hand firmly.

'Then why did you throw your basket into the water and run for dear life down that slope? Do you have such an affinity with the oak and ash that you were merely resting against them, or were you actually collecting your wits and breath as the hunt took place around you?'

She glared at his hand as she tried to think of any argument she could put forward to defend her actions, but she could not.

He let go and folded his arms across his shirted chest. 'I will not apologise, if that is what you expect, when I have clearly rescued you from a predicament when you were hooked to the bank.'

She knew he had seen too much for her to lie and cover her behaviour with a credible tale. Laura had run, as had he; but who he was, dressed in fine trousers and boots, running in a shirt that should have been under a decent man's coat, was a mystery to her. His language was educated, with no hint of a local accent, and his stature bold; but he had been the hunted, not a gentleman hunter. It did not make any sense to her. Inside her head, she could only acknowledge that she was intrigued.

A feeble voice emerged from the gap behind the boulder. 'Daniel, is that you?'

'Ssh, boy! Yes, it is, and I have brought help with me. You shall not be left alone, and you will have food for your empty belly soon enough. So take heart.'

'Thank you, Mr Daniel!' the voice exclaimed.

Laura thought the voice was that of one much younger than the mature man before her.

'Come into the light so our friend can see you,' the man called Daniel said, and Laura watched as a small figure emerged slowly from the shadows. His face was young and gaunt, his right eye swollen, and his arm strapped to his side with a belt. Around his shoulders was a coat that was clearly too big for him — Daniel's, Laura presumed, as the older man smiled reassuringly at the lad who must have been about twelve summers in age, Laura guessed.

'Who are you?' Laura asked. Her eyes were on the bruised figure who leaned precariously against the rock in front of her.

'I'm Jeb Flitch, miss. I fled from the mill over at Gorebeck. I was hurt, and they were going to make me go back under the machines, collecting the bits that fall to the floor and can tangle up the workings. I . . . I was too scared. They own me and I have run . . . I'll be hunted if they get me back, I'll be flogged, or . . . '

'Enough, Jeb. I made you a promise and I shall keep it. But you must rest and stay out of their way. This lady, I believe, will help you. Then I can sort things out so that you do not need to return to that place or spend your life running from them.' Daniel looked at Laura's bemused face. 'Well, miss, what do you say?'

'Well, what? I do not know who you are, or who you think I am that would make you believe that I can help you.' She swallowed as he moved slightly toward her.

'Do not fear me,' he answered her gesture. 'I really am trying to help, that is all. I may have some influence at the mill, but I need to talk to them before they find the lad and punish him, for I believe they will be harsh. Runners are discouraged, and that is why I need to talk to the owner of the mill first, before he is found and returned.'

'I fear no man!' Laura snapped the words out before her head had thought through what she was actually saying.

'Then you should do, for there are many who are dangerous and would seek to . . . Especially if they found such a pretty maid pinned to the bank by her raised skirts.'

Laura coloured deeply. She had been overtaken by events and had not thought what a sight she must have revealed to this stranger.

'Look, we waste time. Are you with us or not?' He seemed anxious to get away, she thought.

Laura straightened her back to hide the shame she felt at being at liberty with a strange man in the woods. 'Why would they listen to you? What position do you hold? You are also a 'runner', are you not? Or do you normally scurry around in bushes and down banks?'

A flicker of a smile crossed his lips before he calmly explained, 'I am the owner's cousin, Mr Daniel Tranton. We have different opinions on some issues, and I hope to break his harsh rules and have him allow me to take the boy on at my own mill.'

Laura looked at him. 'You too are a mill owner?'

Daniel nodded, and Laura saw that she was indeed talking to a man of some wealth and position. 'Help him?' he queried.

'I have little enough money to live on. My father is a fisherman and my mother not from a wealthy family. I cannot do much, but you obviously can.'

'If he is a fisherman, then you have fish aplenty at this time of year. I only ask that you keep his secret here; you clearly have the freedom to wander this area unchaperoned on people's property. You also have the knowledge, mind and ability to trespass and collect food — when you do not throw your gatherings to the wind, that is.'

Laura had risked her liberty for those plants, and now found herself in a real predicament — and, for once, at a loss for words.

'He needs a blanket and some food, and must hide here for a few hours until I can return,' Daniel added.

'Why would you trust him to my care?' she asked. Her mind was spinning as it tried to comprehend what she was being asked to become involved in. If she took this child in, was she also breaking the law? Yet if she left him here to be found, then she was no better than the man who had injured him, or who sent him back to grovel on the floor collecting bits of cloth and thread from under a machine.

Daniel half-smiled at her. 'Because, Miss Laura Pennington, I know you are the daughter of Pennington's fisheries, and I doubt that Obadiah would see a young lad starve. If he doubts your actions, tell him that Mr Daniel Tranton has placed him in your care. He will not query it.'

'How can you speak so? You do not know him . . . do you?'

'I cannot be seen in the town, as I should not be involved in this escapade. I saw the hare was almost caught, and took to the woods myself in order to throw them off his tail. I must return to the mill and see if I can deal with the issue. But it is essential they have no knowledge of my involvement at this point. The legal rights are with Roderick and his men, and I do not wish this to become embroiled in a battle of property between myself and my cousin. We have larger issues to face than the plight of one hapless lad. But that does not mean I will stand back and let one be hunted like a fox. I would prefer to find a more amicable settlement. Roderick is a competitive man, and he does not hold with the bills being pushed in Parliament about ten hours being an adequate working day — I do, and have already reduced the shifts accordingly. I also have shorter hours for children.'

'What of the morality?'

'The moral arguments are ones that are not for us to debate at present, and it would not help Jeb now if we did, would it? So our meeting was fortuitous, because now I do not need to venture into Ebton and risk being seen, and instead can make haste to Gorebeck.'

'If you know who I am, then how so? Do you know my father?' Laura's stern countenance seemed to amuse the stranger until he saw the lad beginning to sink at the knees. He scooped him up in his arms as if he weighed no more than a babe. She could not fathom how this stranger should speak so informally to her as if they were already family acquaintances. Yet she had not even heard his name before. The Gorebeck Mill, though, was known; its reputation almost as bleak as that of the poorhouse.

'I will help him, but I cannot carry him,' she said. 'You will have to stay here a while longer. I will go and fetch some food, a blanket, and my father if he has returned. Then, Mr Daniel Tranton, you can explain yourself to him.'

'Very well. But, Miss Laura, how will you explain that you were on their land?'

'That is an issue I will deal with.' Laura's confidence returned, for when it came to facing her father she had no fears. The man was just; and, what was more, he loved her dearly. He would understand, because she shared his spirit. Her mother, however, did not, and she could become a problem if she knew what was happening.

Daniel nodded and took the lad back inside the shelter of her childhood hiding place. 'Be quick about it, though. He is cold and hungry.'

His voice lingered on the air as Laura ran back down the path that led to her home. She wondered what she would actually tell her father, for he would be more than disappointed in her. She did not fear him, but she hated to let him down or to bring him shame after he had worked so hard to establish a good reputation for the name of Pennington.

She had once again walked off on her own onto the estate lands, despite being warned from her childhood never to go there. She quickened her step as she neared the bank that would lead her to her home. The poor lad — he was so thin. She would feed him up and bring salve. Then, as she looked across the sandy bay, she wondered if he had ever seen the sea. If she did not act quickly, he may not yet.

4

Laura entered her home by the tall green door. It was newly painted, like everything inside; her mother wanted it fresh. There were no more stone-flagged floors, as in their old cottage; instead, they lived in grand style like the townsfolk in the market town of Gorebeck over the moor. The newly laid carpet stretched out before her, the fanlight above the door allowing the sun to shine directly into the painted hallway. She loved the pastel shade of yellow that brightened the narrow corridor. The white door surrounds led to four different rooms: blue for the morning room, green for the library, cream for the drawing room and aqua for the dining room. Mrs Gladys Pennington had created her ideal home, and no one criticised or questioned her taste. Fortunately, she did not have many callers from over the moor who could discern what was apt and what was not. The local people had similar tastes, those who could afford to live in the newer housing along the terrace.

This home was spacious and had three floors to it. The servants — a housemaid, cook and scullery maid — had the sparse highest level, and the family the lower two. Mrs Pennington hoped that when they could afford a carriage they would have a liveried groom and stable lad, but her sea-loving husband had no interest in such a waste of his money. It was one battle Laura doubted that even her mother could win. But the empty stall that had been used as a boathouse temporarily did give Laura an idea.

She was relieved to see their housemaid, Annie Biggs, in the hallway. To her mother and father, she was always just 'Biggs', but Laura objected to this. When the two young women were together, they tended to resort to how they had been as childhood playmates, though Laura was finding it more and more difficult to cope with the dual of roles of mistress and friend.

Annie used to play with her as a child when they both lived in the old hamlet, before Mr Pennington had become rich. Then he had had only a small fishing boat — a coble, like all the other fishermen — but he had one thing they did not: the ability to see an opportunity when it crossed his path. When the smuggling that had supplemented the townships on this northeast section of coast died out, Obadiah saw the town changing and knew that he had to fill a void, or people would go hungry again, because fish and crops had seasons. One bad season of crops from the land and poor catches at sea if the fish did not come, and the villagers went hungry. The money from contraband had kept the local economy afloat, so Pennington had thought fast and recreated the town as he would have it.

New roads brought people nearer. They now came from the colliery towns, places that were more crowded and far dirtier than the farming villages many of them grew from. So they sought out a healthier, fresher climate. Just like the thriving spa towns of Harrogate and Scarborough, Ebton was also becoming a place to bathe and take the fresh air — although it was often quite cold. This was the north-east coast of England, not the south coast of France. Even the cold air was supposed to be good for the body as it cleansed the bad humours — or so Mr Pennington said. He had helped to spread the tales of its miraculous properties far and wide, knowing that a strong conviction could sell a story as much as the smell of a good baker's oven would sell a loaf. One just had to keep the tongues wagging with fresh ideas and tales.

Laura's father was one to see that where there was a desire, there was also an opportunity to do trade. He had been to Scarborough, seen an unusual contraption, and copied it. He offered the use of Ebton's first bathing machine: this was a success which led to the purchase of three more. Then he offered trips along the coast to the bay towns further south. He filled the trippers' heads with further tales of the benefits of eating the freshly caught and dressed Whitby crabs, and the various catches that could be eaten there. Then, of course, he led them to a place that bought their fish from one of his boats.

For the more daring, he even ran fishing trips. Soon Pennington had five boats, and was also running a small, respectable hotel in town with Mrs Myrtle King, the widowed landlady who supervised a clean and friendly house. He had great ideas beyond the hard and seasonal life of a fisherman. His vision was providing work for many in the communities along the bay. Fishing still had its place, but so did his other ventures. Now they had been able to afford one of the new houses on the cliff to live in by themselves.

Laura looked around her at the new,

almost untouched home, and felt sad. The cottage of her childhood had always been lived in, with neighbours coming and going. The sand had been a constant presence, as its fine grains were always being blown in, and had to be swept out on a daily basis. Here, though, people only came if they were expected, and the sand was left outside below the cliff on the beach of the old town. Her mother had also changed, though. Admittedly, she was never one to laugh or sing, but she had become increasingly dour and removed from the people who had once been her friends and neighbours. She read about what was expected of a lady, learnt how to run a 'proper' house, and now absorbed herself in the problems associated with raising a daughter fit to be 'brought out' in society and finding a suitable husband.

This idea shocked Laura, because they had never mixed in any 'society' other than their own. She was sure that any type of gentry born to such a rank would instantly smell fish on their hands as they entered any assembly rooms for any dance. Annie's father, meanwhile, still toiled hard as a fisherman in the small village below on the sandy shore, nestled under the ancient three-hundred-foot-high headland of Stangcliffe, but the boat was not his anymore; it was rented from Pennington, just as his cottage was.

'Where's Father, Annie?' Laura whispered, glancing into the morning room as she passed by.

'I think he is in the shipyard, and won't be back till late. He said to forget his dinner, but to leave him a cold platter for his suppertime.' She must have seen the disappointment on Laura's face, so added, 'Miss, your mother is in there, reading.' Annie gestured to the open doorway.

Laura was disappointed. She had so wanted to seek his help and advice. The man called Daniel Tranton had saved a lad, and then was prepared to leave him with a total stranger. Her father kept himself busy, but Laura felt there was more to it than sheer demand. It was as if he would keep away from the house, or his wife, as often as he could. When he returned, Mrs Pennington often had a list of things he had neglected and plans for social gatherings that he was ill-equipped to attend. But her father was a charismatic man whose enthusiasm for life and desire to constantly invent the new made him something bordering an eccentric character known throughout the sweeping bay towns that their world consisted of. On the few times he had attended a formal event, his bravado and confidence had either won the people over, or at the very least amused them and given them something to talk about to Gorebeck and beyond. Laura wondered if this was how Daniel had come to know of him.

'Biggs, is that you?' Mrs Pennington's voice echoed around the hall.

'Yes, ma'am,' she answered.

Laura shook her head to tell Annie that she did not want to make her return known. The last person she wanted involved in her latest and most daring adventure yet would be her mother. If she heard about a runaway, she would call the militia in; and then, having ordered them to do their duty and secure the town, would take to her bed with the burden of it all. Mrs Pennington was not a lady to underplay a drama.

'Then stop loitering, girl, and bring me some tea. I have such a thirst — no doubt having to shout at you has caused it. Can you not come to me when I ring the bell?'

Annie walked calmly into the room; she dipped a little curtsey to the rather large figure of Mrs Pennington as she sat watching the world go by in the town below from her window seat. It seemed to give her a feeling of grandeur to be above it all.

'I'll bring your tea shortly, ma'am. I did not hear the bell. Perhaps it needs fixing again.'

'Good heavens! Do you seek to tell

me what needs doing now? And you a flibbertigibbet of a lass, no older than my own daughter! Where were you? Not wasting your time and our money dallying by the beach, I hope. Now that I mention her, where is my daughter? I have not seen her today.'

'She went on an errand this morning, I believe,' Annie lied.

'I will speak to Mr Pennington about this. She is not his errand boy. The man has no idea how hard it is to find that girl a suitor. Goodness, is our only child to be left here, an old maid? She would have the hands and manners of a common fisherwoman if it was left to him.'

Laura was looking through the door jamb, and cringed at her mother's words. She noticed Annie's hand form a ball as she listened, even though her face remained impassive; for her mother, Ivy, was a fisherwoman and had a good heart. It was not that many years ago that she had been welcome in the Penningtons' cottage.

'Who will look after her when I go to

heaven?' Mrs Pennington dabbed a lace handkerchief to her forehead and sniffed. 'For I will, one day, and that selfish girl never stops to think of the time when I will not be here. Instead, she ignores me. I will need a companion, soon as I have not had her company for so long.'

'I am sure, ma'am, but she is an early riser and finds many things to occupy herself with.' Annie stepped back a little as Mrs Pennington's face changed from self-pity to anger in a trice.

'You are not paid to think, girl, and if I seek your opinion then I shall ask it. You girls have no thought for the wisdom of your parents. We look to the future whilst you wallow in your present. She must marry! Her cousin will inherit all our wealth if she does not, and then our work will have been for nothing. That's who'll take over my home from us if anything happens to Mr Pennington — Mr Reginald Blagdon and his insufferable wife, Amelia. She is an uncharitable woman if ever I have known one, and, I suspect, has French blood running in her fickle veins.' The heated tone of her voice subsided as she must have realised her thoughts had run off too fast with her tongue. 'Biggs, get me that tea and stop wasting my time!'

'Yes, ma'am,' Annie said, and left the room closing the door quietly behind her. Her eyes flicked upwards to the ceiling as she let out a low breath. She looked at Laura, who had moved away and was trying to cover her shock at the content of her mother's outburst.

'Well, Miss Laura, I for one was not expecting that! Am I an old maid too? Do I have the hands and manners of a common fisherwoman? I am not meant to think? Well, that's news to me. I'm glad she allows me to breathe, but then I'd have difficulty fetching and carrying for her if I didn't, so she'd care about that!' Annie's cheeks were high in colour.

Laura bit her lip. This was awkward. As her friend, she felt sorry for the girl's hurt. She knew how much Annie had dreamed of marrying one of the fishermen's sons, Sidney Bass; but he had wed Alice Johns not two month since, leaving Annie nursing a broken heart and a shattered dream. However, Annie should not speak that way to Laura, especially about her own mother. Her position was one that should mean she kept her thoughts to herself. But Laura had not the heart to rebuke her, especially when she needed her help — at the very least as a loyal servant, if not as a good friend.

Laura shook her head. 'Mama talks out of frustration. She is lonely and has too much time to think. Please be tolerant of her. You are happy working here, aren't you?'

Annie looked at her and then at the new shoes she had been given as part of her uniform. 'I do not mean to appear ungrateful. You know I need this job; it makes life easier for Mother as she has worked so hard for so long. Her hands do need a rest now or they will be unable to do simple tasks. The cold makes her knuckles sore and her hands become swollen. It's just your mother takes on so, and puts me down in such a high-handed way, and never asks after mine. They used to share time together, eating and drinking as friends. Now it is as if my ma is dead to yours, and that hurts her. She is always asking after Gladys; what am I to say? Then, well, I thought Sid and me had an understanding, and yet he went off with Alice. Why?' She sniffed and wiped her eyes on the back of her sleeve. 'We kissed, Laura. I thought that meant that we were walking out properly.'

Laura took Annie's arm gently by the elbow and led her along the hall to the servants' stairwell. 'Annie, was that all you did?' she asked, thinking it was quite enough really.

'Yes! What do you think of me? I should never have said anything. I'm not a dollymop! Do you look for gossip to spread around your newfound friends?'

Laura looked at her. 'What friends?' These sad words were her instant reply, because she had met people when they called, but none of them she would call a friend. Then she added, 'You're not a — what?'

'I am not a fallen woman, if that is what you think of me.'

'No, I don't. Of course not. I meant, if the beast had pressed you to . . . well, you know . . . then he should be . . . ' Laura was rapidly sinking out of her depth, and time was passing.

Annie stepped toward the stairs. 'Oh, Laura, you have much to learn in life.'

Laura almost panicked, realising that she had become sidetracked from her task, and thinking of Daniel waiting for her. His deep brown eyes would be cross, she thought, and pondered what a lovely colour they were — like dark chocolate. Then, realising she had drifted again, she suddenly announced: 'I need two warm blankets, strips of clean cloth, salve, bread, ham, and ale or milk. I will go and find a lamp.

Please be quick and discreet, Annie.' Laura thought that the note of authority in her voice would work, but it did not.

Annie did not move. 'What are you about, Miss Laura Pennington?' Her curiosity cut across her previous indignation.

Laura did not care for the sarcastic tone in Annie's voice. 'That is none of your concern, Biggs.' Laura tried to sound firm with her lowered voice.

However, Annie, who had now fully recovered from her upset, looked straight back at her with a determined stance that told Laura she was not going to do as she was ordered without further explanation. She raised one eyebrow. 'I've just remembered I have to see to the mistress's tea, so I've no time to stand here gossiping.'

Laura swore to herself in frustration. She had allowed this woman to know her too well as a girl, and had taken her in as a maid thinking they could be friends still, before understanding that she was creating another problem for herself. There was no clear barrier between the two ranks, and so it was difficult for Laura to know how to act and react to her.

'Annie, please, I . . . '

Annie sighed. 'I have already told a lie for you once today, Laura. If you are hiding something, or someone, and you want my help to take things from this house, then you had better tell me who and why, because my position is at risk if I am found out — whereas you would get away with an ear-bashing or being married off, miss.' Annie's voice was not malicious, but rather, brutally honest.

Laura nodded. 'There is a hurt boy who needs my help, just for a few hours. Please, I must hurry — and thank you for covering for me with Mother.'

Annie smiled. 'I will have to sort Mrs Pennington out first, but if you wait for me by the yard door, I will bring the bundle there. But Laura, you take care.

I heard gunshots earlier, and there is no gamekeeper on the estate today. I'd know, because Abel is a beater when the hunt is on, and he has gone with the master of the big house over to Gorebeck Moor today. I hope your help does not involve anyone bad?' She raised her eyebrow again; it was a habit she had, and it usually worked, but Laura wanted to waste no more time. It was because Annie was a friend and needed her job that Laura did not want to involve her further; besides, if she confided in her mother, the whole of Ebton would know that Jeb was being hidden by the Penningtons. The whole thing was a mess, and she wished that she had never laid eyes on the handsome face of Mr Daniel Tranton — or, at least, she thought she should wish that.

5

Half an hour later, Laura walked around the back of the tall buildings as if she were admiring the view, and tried to keep an even gait so that she did not appear rushed to anyone taking the air along the top promenade. The moment she slipped into the alleyway between the terraces, she quickened her step and put the hood of her cloak up to cover her head. She wanted to be invisible to the world, as if the quest she was now on was nothing to do with Miss Laura Pennington, but instead the person she was temporarily being — a very daring young woman.

Laura was delighted to find that Annie was waiting for her. Her friend was smiling, though, as if she were amused by something.

'What are you so happy about, Annie?' Laura asked, glancing behind her; but there was no one else there.

'You, miss. Why are you wrapped up so warm when the day is so bright and sunny?'

Annie was taken aback by Laura's snapped reply: 'I do not wish to be seen!'

'Laura,' Annie said, softening her voice, 'you will stand out whether you use a cloak to hide the bundle or boldly march it along the promenade. You are not a maidservant, so whatever would folk think of you carrying such a burden?'

Laura realised she had an excellent point — but what to do? 'Well, I have no choice. Someone needs my help, and I have given my word that I will not abandon them.' She bit her lip as if to prevent any further information slipping out.

'Find the doctor, or take him down to the village — he'd help a lad in trouble. I do not know what you have got yourself involved with, Laura, or why, but I do not want either of us to end up in trouble. Where are you going?'

Laura hedged for a moment. How much was safe to say? And yet time was pressing. 'I need to slip unnoticed into the woods.' She looked down the back street, which was thankfully empty. 'It is better that you do not ask me any more.'

'You go to the gardens behind the old village, and I will meet you by the woodland at the back. But, Laura, this will cost you a new ribbon if all goes well; and if I end up in bother, you will have to see me right,' Annie said, holding firm to the bundle.

'Very well,' Laura said. She walked at a pace in the direction of the steep bank that led down to the old village, her cloak billowing noticeably behind her as she made her way down.

* * *

Annie used an old path that was considered too steep for the gentlefolk to use, and met Laura by the edge of the woods.

'Thank you for doing this; I will have words with Mother about seeing yours.' Laura smiled.

'Aye, well, if you can put that right, then I'll believe them pigs really can fly. Take care.'

Laura took the bundle, holding it firmly under her arm beneath the cloak. She disappeared into the cover of the trees and made her way as quickly as she could back to Daniel and the boy, Jeb.

* * *

'Thank goodness you have returned. I had begun to wonder if you had become too scared.' Daniel took the things from her, and the lamp, which he lit in a moment. Without speaking a word, he gave the boy the food and flask, and then stepped around Laura as if he were going to leave by slipping back through the opening.

'When I give my word, I keep it. I told you, I am not scared of any man.' Laura spoke with conviction, and he nodded this time instead of offering a rebuke.

'I hope you never have cause to be. You saw the wisdom of not bothering your father. That is just as well, as I do not want his reputation sullied in any way. I admire the man for achieving all he has in life. Besides, there is a matter between us that is not as clear as I thought it should be. Are you aware of it?'

'Am I aware of what?'

He studied her for a moment as if he were expecting her to say more.

'What is it? If you are in such a rush, then please speak your mind. I do not like riddles.' Laura felt vexed with him. He seemed to be controlling her life and spoiling her already threatened freedom.

'Very well. Have you seen me before — in Gorebeck, perhaps?' he asked.

'No, I have never set eyes on you

before you grabbed me so boldly in the gill.'

'Have you heard of me, perhaps at the assembly rooms in Gorebeck?' He continued with his annoying, and seemingly irrelevant, questioning.

Laura was amazed at the man's obsession with his own reputation. Did he really think that every young maid in the district knew of him? 'No! Why should I?' Laura persisted.

'Then you know of no letter or arrangement?' He stood before her, staring down as if he were trying to fathom something within her words that simply was not there.

For a moment Laura was transfixed as he held her gaze, each looking into the depth of the other's soul, seemingly trying to stare the other down. It was as if it were she who was playing a game with him, though he was blatantly toying with her. 'I only know that, for a man who has so much pressure on his time, you seem to have plenty to ask nonsensical questions.'

'Very well. As I said, I would not want to damage your father's reputation.' He looked at Jeb, but his mind seemed elsewhere.

'But mine does not matter?' she queried, trying to keep the note of indignation in her voice. If he could take the time to find out if his reputation, whatever it was, had travelled as far as the coast, then she could take the time to knock it down. Laura had also a reputation and family name to uphold.

'Yours? Well . . . I do not wish to sound indelicate, but Miss Pennington, you had already played dangerous games with your own reputation by trespassing on another man's land, on your own, and getting yourself nearly shot in the process. You are fortunate it was I who found you pinned to the bank, your skirts pulled awry. Otherwise, more than your reputation could have been lost to you. Then no man would even look at you as a marital prospect.'

Laura was shocked at the blunt way he described her predicament. It seemed a personal attack upon her character, and was crude in its delivery. 'How dare you?'

'Do you not see? You could have been in a very perilous situation through your own doing. What lady would crawl around in the dirt like that?' His manner had changed.

Laura wanted to slap his arrogant face, but she had never before hit out at anyone, let alone a stranger. Did he seek to ruin her reputation? Was he going to hold it against her? She decided to answer as she felt a lady should. 'If you think so little of me, then I will bid you good day. You have taken the care of this boy on yourself; you can see him right. I will trouble you no more.' This time it was she who turned to slip from behind the rock and back into the wooded gill.

He took hold of her arm and pulled her nearer to him. 'I am not trying to belittle you, Miss Pennington — Miss

Laura — for it would not be in my interest to do such a thing if your father's offer is in earnest. I am trying to make you see the danger in which you placed yourself. You are no child, but a beautiful young woman. I merely point out to someone who is very naive that what you did was ill-advised at the very least, and you should seek instead to humour yourself in the house and be more wary of walking on your own on another's property. You have spirit and are an attractive young woman, but that can be spoilt so easily if you cross the path of a man who is no gentleman — and who would be ruined most then?'

Laura was going to retort, but Jeb coughed and so she fell silent. Daniel's words were true; but more than that, he had described her as beautiful and attractive. Yet she had always thought herself to be a commoner, and here he was a gentleman declaring these words to her. Then she was jolted back to reality as he spoke different words that filled her with fear.

'I shall only be a few hours; but if you stay here, I will return before dark and take him to a safer place.' He moved as if to leave.

Laura was overcome by a wave of panic, and this time it was she who reached out, grabbing hold of his sleeve. She was not sure which of them looked more surprised. Instantly, she let go of him.

'Please, I must be home soon.' She looked at those eyes and knew that she would do as he bid her, putting pride aside, as there was a young life in need of sustenance who had been wronged in some cruel way. But how she would explain to her mother where she had been, goodness only knew.

'Stay with Jeb, please.' He placed a hand on her shoulder, and this time she did not pull away from him. His eyes held hers. 'They have put a price on him, so do not decide to trust the villagers and ask for help. They would turn the stranger in without it pricking their consciences.'

'They are kind people,' Laura added defensively.

He smiled at her. 'Then you see the good in everyone. They are hardy people who have a harsh life, existing on a rough shore with a seasonal income and many changes. Do you think they all admire your father? Don't you think some will resent his success on the back of their loss of a less worthy occupation — smuggling?'

'My father is respected and loved.' She watched as Daniel gently shook his head and removed his hand.

'Laura, stay or go; but you hold a boy's life in your hands, and I believe you have a conscience. Take my advice and do not reveal his presence to those villagers. You will be worldlier one day; but for now, accept that what I tell you is meant to save pain, and not to upset your strong and admirable sense of loyalty.' Without waiting for a reply, he left.

Laura stood transfixed for a moment

as she fathomed the depth of his message. Was her father loved, or loathed? Did her mother's high-handedness undermine all that her father had achieved in creating the success of the town? Had he been seen as someone who was splitting the old town from the new? If so, what else was true that Laura had never realised? She stood straight and decided that as soon as she had dealt with this problem that had been set before her, she would set time aside and have another good chat with Annie.

6

'You don't have to stay, miss.' The feeble voice almost echoed around the earthen walls of this old smugglers' place for their hidden stash. Tub-men would pick up kegs and take them from there across the moors to Gorebeck and the manors round about. The evidence of what it was once used for was still there, with a small keg left abandoned.

Laura pulled it over to where Jeb was lying down wrapped in the blankets. He had eaten his fill. She unwrapped the cloth around the small jar of salve. Annie had thoughtfully included a small bottle of vinegar and placed an offcut of muslin next to it.

'You have a graze on your arm. I would like to see it; and whilst we have the lamplight, now would be a good time.'

The lad inched himself up to a sitting

position and gingerly pulled off his rough-cut jacket. He cringed as Laura eased the jacket's fabric from his shirt. Then she slipped him out of the dirty shirt that clung to his skin around the cut. Taking the muslin and the vinegar, she began cleaning the fragments of cloth away, and then the cut itself. It was about two inches, and although it was deeper at one end than the other, when she looked it seemed to be a clean wound. Jeb grimaced as the vinegar stung. Once this was done she removed his shirt and could clearly see that he had been bruised also. Marks on his back looked older, as if he had been struck by a stick. This convinced her that she would help him. Silently she applied the salve to the wound and then wrapped the clean cloth around it to hold it in place.

'If your friend Mr Tranton does not return within the next few hours, I will have to leave you for a while, for I will be missed; but I will return under the cover of darkness, and then I will smuggle you into my home.'

Jeb's eyes widened. 'Why would you do so much for the likes of me? You is gentry; I'm nothing!'

Laura could not help letting a small laugh escape her lips, although his words, in essence, were not funny. 'We may live well enough now, but there was a time . . . never mind. You should never say you are nothing — everyone is someone. I am only doing my Christian duty and helping you as you are hurt.'

'Thank you,' he said quietly, then added, 'Many would not look my way, Christian or not. My fate is my own. You think he is my friend, then?'

Laura was surprised. 'Mr Tranton? Don't you?'

'He is one of the family of mill owners, and they only think of what is good for their wallets. He is Mr Roderick's cousin and owns another mill. Folk say it is better, but that don't mean it is good. All them machines are monsters. The noise they make could have been born from the eggs of dragons, they are so evil. Then there is the bits of fluff that get in your eyes, hair and on your chest. They make me cough.'

'You really are scared of the place, aren't you?' Laura asked, and watched the lad nod his head.

'Perhaps he just wanted to take the credit for returning me himself. I mean, why not take me back with him if he can get my papers?' Jeb was eased back into his shirt and jacket. 'He don't like Mr Bullman, so I don't think he would want the man to catch me. Then he'd get Mr Roderick's favour for my return, and I'd get a beating. If Mr Tranton has me mended, then he might have someone new for his own mill who is owing him their life. Either way, he wins.'

'You have a sharp mind, Jeb, if not too cynical for one so young. But why would Mr Tranton risk being shot at if he were not telling us the truth?' Laura asked as she sat on the upturned keg as if it was a stool, chatting to her new friend. For he was in need of her help; and that meant, in her eyes anyway, that he was a friend indeed.

'They like hunting, and there is such competition — gentry, that is. Between them they are always competing. Gentry is funny; they have the taste for blood, even risking their own on a bet. No offence, miss.'

'None taken, Jeb. Like I said, we were not born to the 'gentry', as you call them.'

Laura thought for a moment. She didn't like the idea of being stranded in the place. Certainly she had no intention of being left there into the evening hours. So she pondered what to do with the lad. Then she had an idea. 'Do you think you can walk a mile with me now that you have eaten?' she asked, and saw the fear in Jeb's eyes as he considered her words.

'I'd be recognised.'

'Not if you were with me as my maid,' Laura answered and smiled.

'Think I look too like a man for that,' he said, his voice deepening as if to convince her.

'Not if you wear my cloak and follow at my side.' She looked at his face in the flickering light and saw a glimmer of a smile cross his lips.

'But your folks, what would they say if they saw me enter your home? The servants would talk. Nah, it is kind, miss, but I know folk; they wag their tongues. And I have a price on me. Perhaps if you get one of the fishermen to take me on — ?'

'In your condition? I think not. Look, we have a stable built for a horse and carriage, though as yet we do not have one because my father prefers cobles.'

'He likes stones?' His face twisted as he clearly did not understand. 'Don't see the connection, miss.'

'Not cobblestones! Cobles — that is what the fishing boats are known as. My father prefers being on the water rather than being jolted along in a carriage. We have an unused one, a boat, in the empty stable. It needs fixing, as it leaks, and he has been meaning to see to it for nearly four months. We can hide you in there. That way I can get you some hot food, and you can sleep knowing that nothing, neither man nor beast, will disturb your slumber.'

'But Mr Tranton won't know where to find me.' He looked slightly panicked by the suggestion. 'You think he is my friend, don't you?'

'He knows my family name. He also must think me stupid to believe that he could retrieve his horse, ride an hour to Gorebeck, seek out and make agreement with his cousin, and return before darkness falls. No, we shall be safer moving you to my home.' Laura was convinced of this. She also realised that if she were discovered here, she would answer to strangers and the authorities, whereas at home she would be answerable to her father, and he would know what to do.

Jeb looked at her. 'I'll go with you. I've never been a maid before.'

There was something about the lad's manner that Laura took to. She did not know what she would tell her father, but once he returned she would seek out his advice. If he knew Mr Daniel Tranton, then he could send word to him. If not, well, the lad might find a home in one of the fishermen's cottages down the coast. If he was so adverse to mill life and had no family, he may as well serve a life on the sea. Her main concern was that the lad's arm did not turn bad because it had been left untended too long.

Once the clouds came over and dulled the bright sunlight, Laura declared it was time to leave. She wrapped the cloak around Jeb, arranged the hood to hide his face, and rolled up the blankets so that he could carry them under his good arm. The effect was to make him look like a more portly maid than he would otherwise have been.

Laura led him up the steep path out of the woods to the west cliff and then to the alley behind the terraces. The only people they passed by were too busy about their daily chores at the end of another hard day's toil to pay the lady and her maid any attention. There was only one incident when a young lad chasing his dog nearly bumped into them, but it was only Jack from the inn. He was more embarrassed than curious, and soon went on his way.

Before the light had faded, Jeb was made comfortable in the bottom of the coble, resting on his folded blankets with an oiled cloth over him to keep him warm. He was quite exhausted from the climb, but at least, Laura thought, he was now safe. Then the rain began. A heavier downpour Laura had rarely seen, but she counted her blessings that she was no longer in the woods, for the climb back up with Jeb would have been nigh-on impossible in that torrent.

7

Daniel rode into Gorebeck, which at its eastern side was still a pretty and growing market town. Crossing the bridge by the Norman church, he followed the road past the old barracks and toward the loop in the river where the mill building loomed high amongst the surrounding trees. He entered the yard and dismounted, handing the reins of his horse to a lad who was crossing the yard.

The lad took them, along with the penny he was given to see to the animal. Daniel knew he had to play his hand carefully. Mr Bullman and his louts were still out, so he made his way directly to the office where he knew Roderick would be ending his day poring over ledgers and no doubt answering letters, running down the calls for reform as springing from rabble-rousing revolutionaries.

Daniel felt guilty for involving the Pennington girl. She was a pretty and foolish young woman who had stupidly wandered onto private land and nearly got herself shot. The Hambletons had only purchased the land the summer before; they had arrived from West Yorkshire and were also representative of 'new money' — that which had been earned rather than inherited. The man was obsessed with privacy after the family had been the target of machine wreckers in their old home. Daniel had called there on a few occasions. He had been amazed when he saw the local tradesmen being escorted onto and off the land. At some expense, the man had erected fences and had two ornate gates built. Each gatepost had a lion atop it, sitting majestically but bearing its teeth toward anyone approaching. Hambleton definitely wanted to send a message to anyone who approached them that strangers were unwelcome.

He thought of Laura Pennington and half-smiled. She had courage and character, but he hoped she would not leave the lad on his own without care. He'd sort Pennington out when he returned, if he had found out what his wayward daughter was up to. Daniel never underestimated the man, but respected him for the way he was able to get the locals to do his bidding. For Obadiah had had no formal education, but he had grafted, and had a certain eye for a good deal that Daniel could not help but admire. Some might be jealous of a man who had raised himself up, but Daniel thought it a most worthy skill.

He approached the office. The door was ajar, and he could hear his cousin tut-tutting and slamming a drawer closed. He was not in a good mood, but then — Daniel smiled — he could not really remember many times when Roderick was. He knocked on the doorframe as Roderick looked up.

'Come in, man,' he said quickly, reluctantly acknowledging Daniel's presence. 'Don't stand about like that; you are a gentleman, not a common labourer. Stand with a straight back, man! Did you learn nothing at the school your parents paid for?'

'I learnt many things, Roderick. Are you still sore because your father cut your education short?' Daniel could not help himself from annoying Roderick, as he was so easy to ruffle; but even he knew it was a foolish thing to do when he wanted his cousin on his side.

'I learnt more at my father's desk about this business than you and your pampered pets will have done in any of the great public schools. Now, what brings you here? Be quick, because I am a busy man.' Roderick dipped his pen in the inkwell and signed a paper with a flurry. He regarded himself as a self-made man, despite the fact that he had inherited the mill from his father before him. Daniel half-smiled. Roderick had so many grudges that he could never be anything other than a very bitter man.

Daniel entered the room casually and

smiled, even though he knew the gesture would not be returned. Looking at the array of papers and petitions on the desk in front of Roderick, he sat down opposite. He could see why his cousin's mood was particularly dark. 'Have you heard of the rally the workers are holding next Sunday on Gorebeck Moor?'

'Heard about it? Of course I've heard about it, man. I tried to get that useless bunch of so-called soldiers down at the barracks to stop it, but will they? My demands go unheard. No, they won't even go to it, as they say it could incite a riot! And why do they think this? Because our foolish government is frightened of a public backlash after that Peterloo fiasco. They should have stood their ground and rid the country of the lot of them. We've gone soft. We fought Bonaparte to stop this sort of thing happening here, and they allow it to go ahead! Revolution is coming, you'll see.' He threw the pen down on the desk.

'Calm yourself, Roderick. Your face

has turned red.' Daniel could see he was not in a mood that would be lenient to the plight of a runaway.

'No wonder. It is my blood that's up; it boils and simmers with every petition these rabble-rousers send me. And that is what will be spilt if these revolutionaries have their way — my blood! Yours too. Don't push this away lightly, my young cousin, because we are all in this together. You have a mill and you are one of us.'

'My mill runs more shifts, and gives my workers better food, clothes and education,' Daniel said proudly.

'Aye, you are part of the problem. You pamper them and give them ideas above their God-given place in this world. How you fund it, I do not know — we are in a recession and a crisis is looming. We have competition, and we have ungrateful wretches who would destroy the very machines that the workforce relies on.' He paused and wiped his forehead with his kerchief. 'So, cousin, you came here to tell me something I already know. It was good to see you again. Please close the door as you leave.'

'Have you retired Mr Bullman and his cronies at last?' Daniel asked innocently.

'No, I have not. But if I find he has been sitting in an alehouse drinking instead of finding the runner, I will do — you'll see. Don't think I am not capable of dismissing whomever I choose to. Was there something else? I'm a busy man, even if you are not.'

'A runner?' Daniel continued, ignoring Roderick's usual rude gestures.

'Aye, a young lad. Flitch is his name. Stupid boy injures himself one day and runs away the next. You'd think he had a death wish.' Roderick sat back in his chair and sighed. 'He will be made an example of when I get my hands on him. Revolutionaries, the lot of them.'

Daniel did not react to his words, but for a fleeting moment almost pitied the man. He was so filled with angst that it looked as though it were eating him away. Daniel thought he appeared tired, and even felt sorry for him for a moment. Roderick had never been good enough in his father's eyes: he was short in stature, plain in looks with thinning hair, and had no natural academic gifts. His saving grace was that he had a head for numbers and found great joy in perusing his ledgers.

'Why send Bullman to chase such a poor catch? Surely your men are better used here. They could be playing cat and mouse with a wretch who will be dead in days anyway.' Daniel spoke his words casually, as if he had no great interest in the matter, privately loathing his own dismissal of a human being in such a high-handed manner. Then, as inspiration hit him, he realised that thinking of Laura and the Hambletons had given him a brilliant idea. He could easily obtain what he sought. 'Will you be going to Hambleton's ball next month? Sarah is a fine young woman; she was quite entertaining when last I visited. I think I shall attend.'

Roderick's face went a slightly deeper shade of red, and Daniel knew that he had hit a nerve. The man almost salivated at the mention of her name, but his eyes bore into Daniel's as he mentioned his visit there. In truth, old man Hambleton had made sure that Sarah was nowhere to be seen during Daniel's stay. He kept her for soirées and dances. She was not to be flaunted in front of any one man in case a rumour of an agreement was started. Old Hambleton wanted to net her a good catch: a husband of either rank or wealth, one that would advance his own ambitions.

'Yes, I am. Why? You're surely not going, are you? You should leave the girl alone, as you have no intention of marrying yet.' Roderick scowled.

Daniel waited a moment before answering, seeing Roderick's anxiety grow, and enjoying playing his hand. Sarah was quite pretty, and delicate in looks and disposition. She was younger than Daniel by a year, and Roderick by five. His cousin had an interest in her — but Daniel was more handsome, and Roderick feared that Sarah had an eye for him. If Daniel went to the ball, he could play on Roderick's fear and try to catch her attention; he would certainly see that that was never on Roderick.

'I might be — or could be persuaded against — going . . . ' Daniel answered.

Roderick let out another sigh. 'Damn you, Daniel. You come here to taunt me. Is that the reason for your unannounced arrival? You have not come about any damned meeting, but to make a play for my intended — for so she will be. I play cards with her father, so don't go giving her any stupid ideas about turning her affections in your direction.'

'Why would I do that?' Daniel said, and smiled.

'What do you want?'

'Close the mill for a day and let your workers attend the rally. Show that we are united in our commitment to take their requests seriously.'

'Demands — they make no requests,'

Roderick snapped.

'Well?'

There was a pause while Roderick thought, but the moment was interrupted when Mr Bullman burst into the office, interrupting their discussion, which instantly angered him. Roderick exploded when the man explained he had heard no word of the boy.

'You could not catch a fish in a dried-up riverbed!' Roderick snapped. 'Get back to work.'

'I've sent the word out that if he is found, a reward will be had.' Bullman smiled at his quick thinking and audacity, after showing open annoyance at being so rebuked.

Roderick's face was now the colour of puce. 'It will bloody well come out of your pocket, man, if he is found, then. Get out of my sight!'

Bullman paled slightly at the last statement, and turned and glowered at Daniel as he left.

Roderick shook his head and let out a long, low breath. He turned to Daniel.

'I'll close it for half a day, and no pay for them.'

Daniel pondered this. 'Half a day and throw in the papers for your runaway. I have a taste for some sport today.'

Roderick considered. 'Very well — but your word, man, that you will decline the Hambletons' Ball and leave Miss Sarah to me.'

'Agreed!' They shook on it. Roderick sent for young Jeb's papers, and had him transferred into Daniel's care until he was of an age to work for pay.

'One more thing, Roderick.'

'I'll not give you any more. You have your lot, now go!' Roderick pointed to the door.

'A word of advice for free,' Daniel answered.

'What?'

'Lose Bullman whilst you still can. He is too comfortable in his shoes, and threatens yours.' Daniel saw Roderick take in his words, but oddly he did not reply.

'Good day,' Daniel said and left. He

stepped outside, smiling, happy that he had achieved more than he had expected to. Bullman watched him as he walked across the cobbles. Then, leaving one of his henchmen outside the gates, the overseer stormed into the mill.

Evening would soon be upon them. Daniel needed to eat, his horse needed to rest, and then he would take the road to the coast and see how his new acquisition was faring — or that was the plan, until thunder clapped and the heavens opened. He turned the collar of his coat up and made for the inn. His new acquisition was going to have to wait; and unfortunately, so was Miss Laura Pennington.

8

'Laura! Is that you?' Laura had tried to enter the house unheard and unseen, but as she past the drawing room doorway, the shrill voice shouted her name.

She composed herself, and smiled before entering the room. 'Yes, Ma, it's me.' She walked over to her mother's winged chair by the warmth of the burning fire and leaned to kiss her powdered cheek, but the woman turned her head away.

'Where have you been?'

'I . . . '

'You should call me 'Mother'; you are not a common girl. And what is that on your shoes? You have walked mud onto my Belgian rug. Whatever next?'

'Sorry, Ma . . . Mother. I'll go straight away and change. Is Father in his study?'

Laura used the word 'study', but in

truth it was more of a bolthole for her father. It had a desk that he used when he must, and books lined the walls — not that he ever read any of them, but he had bought them in a job-lot from a house that was taken by a debtor's creditors. What he did use was his bottle of brandy and the crystal glasses that went with it. His favourite chair by his fire was placed next to a small table, on which lay his knife to do his scrimshaw when he fancied it. This was his link to his past: his father had been a seafaring man on the whalers that went out from Whitby. The knife was one of the few things he had left of his, and he treasured it. Not even Mrs Pennington or Laura would dare move it from its place.

'Your father has neither returned nor sent word to me of his intentions. I am constantly beside myself with worry for the two of you, but you never give a thought for me here, all alone.'

Now was her chance, Laura thought. 'But Mother, you need not be on your own, for only today Annie commented that Ivy was thinking of popping over. You two used to enjoy a good natter together, don't you remember?' Laura saw a bemused expression settle on her mother's face.

'Have you no sense of propriety? Laura, put those dark days behind us. How can I ever forget our temporary misfortune of that time, when you 'natter' with your maid and forget yourself so? We live on the cliff now. Our neighbours are all successful people. We are no longer to associate with the commoners; they now work for us. Ivy would never understand, and should not even think of 'popping over'. Whatever would Mr Simpkins think?'

'He is a busy man, and as our neighbour may just think she has business here — if he thinks about it at all. A friend once should still be a friend always — she has done no wrong. We should share our good fortune.'

'Laura!' Her mother snapped out the word. 'It is not our 'good fortune', but the results of hard work and a clear mind that have changed our circumstances. We have been blessed by fortune because we have earned it. Now that Annie serves us, it would hardly be fitting for me to associate with Ivy. Besides, her husband — who, I may add, is more than willing to while away his hours at the inn — works as a fisherman for your father.'

'I will never understand, Mother, how you can so easily detach yourself from your erstwhile friends and then complain of loneliness. I will go to my bedchamber and change.'

'You will, and not just your clothes. You will change that vile tongue and fisherwoman's attitude. You will respect me and your father, be thankful for your position in life, and aspire to greater things.'

'I am happy as I am.' Laura stood her ground. She was in no mood to back down.

'You will cease to answer me back. I will have you sent somewhere where those rough edges can be smoothed down; and then, my girl, you will do your duty and marry, and give your dear father a Pennington heir.'

Laura's mouth dropped open. She had not expected that, and knew it was within her mother's power to arrange it unless her father stepped in.

'You look like a codfish. Compose yourself. The sooner you are matched to one of the Trantons, the sooner I can sleep sound again, knowing you have not thrown your reputation and your life away. Now go!'

Laura felt as though she had been slapped in the face. So that was why the man had rambled on so about a letter. She was being offered up to him, with no say in the matter. 'When were you going to discuss this with me?'

'When one of them wrote back asking for an introduction. Then we would advise you on how to present yourself so that the engagement could be made formal.' Her mother was staring at the flames of the fire.

'Engagement!' Laura's anxiety rose with her voice.

'Yes; once that is official, it is very costly and difficult for a gentleman to back out of the agreement. By the time your true nature was known, it would be too late for him — whichever one it was that took the bait — to walk away from the prospective marriage.' She smiled.

Laura left before words burst out of her mouth that would certainly have her sent away, never to return unless she were forced into a wedding. She swore her mother was being affected by the medication for her nerves. How could she decide on a marriage without consulting her daughter first? It was one decision too far. It was fashionable to have 'nerves' — but as far as Laura was concerned, a good talking-to and a day down in the old town would do her mother more good than physic. Ivy would set her right. But her father let his wife carry on in her own stifling world of grandeur as if he no longer cared.

Laura ran up the stairs to her room. Something would have to be done, and soon. Looking out of her window, she could see that the sky had darkened early. That meant one thing: a storm was coming. It had been a strange day, and a long one. She had been rescued, coerced, and now was the keeper of a lad who was basically an outlaw. Her father had taken off on one of his trips without a word, and all she could do was wait to speak to him of the nonsense that was coming out of his wife's mouth.

At that moment, her thoughts stopped. Tranton had received a letter — one from her father. Was it genuine, or had her mother actually written it in his place? She must seek out her father and put an end to this nonsense. Who would return first, though — a bemused Mr Daniel Tranton or her wandering father?

* * *

Laura could not sleep. Her mother had been impossible today. She had waited for her father to return, but he had not. She needed to tell him about the boy, and also let him know of her mother's threats to marry her off or send her away. He would never agree to it — to either. Word had been sent that the storm was bad at sea, and his boat had not come back up the coast from Whitby. Mrs Pennington had taken a turn of nerves, deciding that all manner of ill fates had befallen her husband, and so had taken laudanum to help her into her slumber — which resulted in Annie being obliged to settle her for the night like a baby, until she was sound asleep.

Annie slept in the upper room of the house, but did not go to bed till late. Laura was so worried for the boy in the stables that, despite the storm and the thunder, she put on one of her father's oiled greatcoats and his broad-brimmed hat, and went to see him.

'Jeb!' she said as she entered the stable. The rain pelted the building as the thunder rolled above them, each clap seeming louder and nearer than the one before, and then the flashes illuminated the sky as if the gods of old were at war. She prayed her father was safely tucked up in bed in Whitby, and not out at sea on one of his adventures.

The lad's head popped up above the side of the boat. 'Yes, miss. Were you scared?' he asked. His manner was much more relaxed, as if being in the vessel, even one on dry land, gave him comfort. Laura was pleased that he seemed perkier.

'I thought you would be. How is the arm?' She was pleased to see him raise it freely.

'Sore, but better than it was. No, storms don't scare me, 'cause I love the feel in the air. It's fresh, not like the air in the mill. Couldn't abide being trapped in that place, and they even locked us in one night. Only I slipped out before the overseer did.' He pointed to the sky through the doorway. 'This is marvellous, isn't it?' He was grinning from ear to ear and Laura could not help but laugh at him. 'Have Mr Bullman and his men gone now?'

'There is no one searching for you that I know of, including your elusive friend, Mr Daniel Tranton.' She took the vexed note out of her voice when she mentioned his name. Her mother's words had cut her to the core and her anger had turned upon the man who had deserted an injured lad to the keeping of a young lady, leaving both of them in peril. Far from the handsome hero she had earlier decided he was, he had now become a selfish mill-owning brute.

She lightened her thoughts, as Jeb's enthusiasm was infectious. 'Yes, it is marvellous. I brought you some milk and ham. I am sorry that I couldn't find the bread in time.' She passed the food over to him.

'Did you know that there was things stashed in here?' Jeb said, and then appeared surprised when Laura began to climb up.

She was intrigued. Without thinking of what she was doing, the time or the place, she hitched up her skirt and, leaving the heavy coat dripping over the side of the boat, climbed up the steps and into the vessel. 'What things?'

'Here, look: this seat is like a box. You move this top plank bit and underneath there is a space for things.'

'I am sure all boats are like that.' Laura was fascinated as he manoeuvred the wood from the top of the hidden compartment.

'No, they aren't. I knows because before I ended up in the mill, I was raised by my granddad, and he used to have a model of a boat like this, as he worked on them all through his life. This boat is seaworthy. You're wrong about it needing work done.'

'But you didn't know that it was called a coble,' Laura said.

'Sorry, miss, I thought it best not to let on. I love boats, and that is why I came here. I wanted to be in one.'

Laura was surprised by his words, but she did not doubt that what he said was true. So why had her father said that the boat was to be worked on? Unless it was to stop his wife asking again for a carriage and a pair of horses to pull it. 'So what did you find?' she asked, her curiosity roused.

'A pistol, bullets, some money and paper; a fob watch and some dried biscuits. Oh, and a hipflask with what smells like brandy in it. If this vessel needed fixing, I would say the work has been finished a while, and it is certainly being prepared ready for a journey.'

Laura looked at the paper, which was carefully kept in a wallet. It was a bond for a hundred pounds, to be drawn on a bank in the city of London.

'Jeb, you have not taken anything from here.'

The lad looked hurt in the flash of light that illuminated the stables from the open door. 'I'm not a thief. I would not have shown you them if you were going to accuse me of such things.' He struggled with his one good arm to replace the seat. Laura put everything back where it had been found and replaced the lid.

'It was not a question, Jeb. I was making a statement. You are an honest person and I respect that. If what you say is true, then I may have left you in a place where you may be discovered.' Laura yawned; she felt so tired.

'You go back to bed, miss. The storm will take a while to blow over. No one is going to move this tonight. You rest, and tomorrow Mr Tranton will arrive, you'll see. All will be well.'

Laura climbed back down, wrapped herself in the coat, and braced herself for the dash across the yard to the back door. She loved Jeb's renewed spirit and confidence, but somehow did not share his optimism.

9

The rain stopped sometime in the early hours, but the roads beyond the nearby newly laid ones south of Gorebeck, leading to the coast, were a quagmire. Daniel arose after spending the night at the inn, but as he talked to the coach driver who had lumbered into the inn early in the morning, he decided it would be unwise to risk the journey until he was certain the storm had passed by.

News of another nature had been brought to him: the peaceful meeting that was to be held on Gorebeck Moor to address the workers' concerns about the loss of their cottage flax industry and the long, hard hours in the manufactories of cotton was to be usurped by West Yorkshire rebels. These were hard men who preferred deeds to talk, their preferred action being to break the machines in revolt against an unsympathetic government. If this message was to be believed, then Daniel knew the workers would never have any reform granted to them. If they did not die at the rally when soldiers were sent in, then the day they broke a Tranton machine would be the day all hell broke out in the community. Men would be placed in gaol and the mills would run as before, but with bitter distrust.

Somehow Daniel had to stop the troublemakers before they whipped the crowd up into a frenzy of indignation where anything they did would be ill thought out and counterproductive. The boy Jeb would have to wait. He decided to send a letter to Miss Laura, making it clear that he wanted her to keep the lad safe as his apprentice, and that he was no longer a runner. He would put things right with her and offer recompense to her father for the lad's keep, as he was sure that Obadiah would take him in.

Convinced this was the best action,

he set about seeking the quickest way the letter could be delivered before he rode west.

* * *

Laura was up very early despite her late night. She watched the sun rise, dressed, and then made her way carefully downstairs. The grandfather clock in the hall ticked the minutes away. She crept down the servants' corridor and waited for Cook, whose day always began at first light. She needed a kitchen maid, but Mrs Pennington insisted she had not seen one that was suitable. It was part of her mother's way to save as much as she could, and then spend on something grand for the house, such as her carriage.

Cook went down to the stone corridor that separated the dairy from the cold store and then slipped into the room, carrying her jug. Laura ran straight out across the yard and into the stables. There she stopped. She nearly skidded on the wet cobbles as she approached the stable, seeing that the doors were open wide. She walked tentatively inside and strode around the empty space, unable to believe that the coble had gone. It simply could not be so.

'It's vanished,' she muttered to herself. She stared at the ground and saw the marks of two wheels, then noticed a couple of hoof-marks where mud had settled on the flagstone floor. The boat had been moved — and with it, she supposed, Jeb had been pulled out of his safe haven. She had heard no cries for help or remonstrations of innocence. The household had not been disturbed, so perhaps Jeb had not been discovered. Then she thought of the items hidden in the boat and felt fearful of what might have happened to the boy.

She ran back inside the house. This time she was seen by the astonished Cook. 'Whatever are you doing here at this time of day, miss?' She looked around. 'Has something happened to Mr or Mrs Pennington?'

'Cook, someone has stolen Father's boat!' Laura exclaimed.

'No one has stolen anything.' She shook her head. 'Calm yourself. Goodness, I told them to be as quiet as they could, and I thought they had been, so that no one was disturbed. After the rain the going was soft, so it was a good time to move it down the back alley and away. What's a boat doing up on a cliff, anyways?'

'Does Father know? Has he returned?' Laura asked.

Cook gave her a strange look and shook her head. 'Your mother told Annie to fetch her father to take the boat down to the shore and put it next to your father's other ones. She said it had no place there as she had a man coming to look at the 'coach house', as she refers to the stable, miss. The man who is arriving tomorrow sells coaches.'

'But when did they come? Why do it in the night?' Laura was trying to keep up with events.

'Not night. Early this morning.

Fishermen get up early, like your father does.'

Laura ignored the comment in case Cook was trying to remind her of her father's humble beginnings. 'If he comes back, please find me. I must talk to him urgently.'

'Miss, it is their argument; leave it to them. I mean, I would suggest you . . . ' She shrugged as Laura spun around without comment and walked through to the hallway.

She hurriedly took down her coat from the hallstand and pulled it on. Grabbing her hat, she went out of the house and made straight for the old town; but as she stood at the top of the winding bank and looked towards the gill she saw that it too had suffered in the storm. The shoreline was a mass of broken-up vegetation and soil. The heavy rains had caused the beck to flood. She swallowed.

'Thank God I did not stay there. We could have been drowned!' she muttered to herself, as if her own voice could offer comfort. But once again her thoughts were interrupted as she looked to the shoreline. Two fishermen were pushing a boat out to sea: there were another four figures inside it, but she could not tell if it was her family's boat or if Jeb was in it. This day had started as strangely as her previous one had ended.

'Can anything become more confusing or worse than this?' The sun had not long dawned, and she felt tired, but was loath to return to the house so soon. She could not go running down to the old village, as everyone would be waking. Besides, Jeb seemed a quick-thinking lad, and he knew his way back to her if he needed help. This thought offered some comfort, so she wandered along the top of the cliff, enjoying the view and telling herself not to panic. After all, she was not supposed to know that the boat held secrets, and Jeb had said he wanted to be at sea. Besides, it might not be the same boat. Mr Daniel Tranton had abandoned both her and the boy to the elements and their fate.

Opposite, further along the row of high terraced houses, a door opened. It was the door to Pennington's Hotel. Mrs King must have an early riser leaving the establishment, she thought. Laura stepped back into the shelter of the few trees that marked the beginning of the woods to the north of the town. It would not do for her to be seen wandering alone at this hour. Her heart, which had had two shocks already this day, skipped a beat as it had the biggest one yet.

Her father was stepping out of the hotel. This seemed strange, for why would he spend a night in his hotel and not return home to them — his family? He looked around, then quickly leaned back to the proprietress and gave Mrs Myrtle King a kiss on the lips. Not a polite peck — although that would have been bad enough — but a full kiss. Then he quickly spirited himself away and walked briskly back towards the newly painted door of his home.

Laura leaned against a tree and stilled herself whilst her heart slowly but surely began to break. He had not been at sea in the storm. He had been a few doors away and cavorting with Mrs Myrtle King. Her father was an adulterer! She could cry, she could scream, and she could accuse her father of being totally selfish . . . but all she really wanted to do was to run to him and ask him to explain. Like a child, she did not want this to be true. But she realised that it was so, because what was there for him to come home to? A cold and indifferent wife and a self-absorbed, wandering daughter. Would she end up like him?

She breathed deeply and headed home. He had always been straight with her, and she had never feared him. Now was a time to talk, not shout. He was about to discover that his wife had taken matters into her own hands and moved his precious boat — and, unwittingly, with it a lad and a private stash of valuables.

* * *

Laura followed her father into the house. She saw him entering his office as she slipped inside the hallway. Leaving her hat and coat on the walnut hallstand, she headed straight into the room after him. There he calmly sat, the man she had admired, loved and looked up to all her life, casually pouring his glass of brandy and placing it on the table next to his scrimshaw-handled knife.

He looked up at the doorway as she entered. 'Close the door after you, Laura, and keep the warmth of the fire inside the room with us. It is very fresh out there after the storm.' He glanced at her. 'You rise before the sun has had a chance to even warm the air.'

She swallowed and did as he bid her, then stood before him, staring down at his tired eyes, hoping he would offer up a word of explanation before she had to confront him.

'You have something on your mind,

Laura?' His words, softly spoken, were challenging her to say her piece or leave.

'I saw you,' she said.

'Good. You often do. And I saw you, young lady, walking onto Hambleton's land after I forbade it.' He stared at her, but she did not avert her eyes.

'That's as may be. But Father, I saw you!' Her voice rose slightly, partly to offset the instant pang of guilt, but mainly because she could not believe he would carry on with the King woman not two doors from their home.

'When in particular did you see me?' He stared at her; his eyes were not warm like they normally were. Instead, they almost looked dismayed.

'Just now. I saw you kiss Mrs King!' Her voice had risen again and she was struggling to keep it controlled.

'You did, did you? And what would you be doing up and out on the street at this hour of the day on your own?' There was no sign or sound of remorse or shock in his voice, more a resigned note of fate. However, his concern for her safety was obvious.

Undeterred, she was determined not to let him off by diverting blame onto her. 'I was looking at your boat on the waves and trying to see if you returned to us safely after the storm. Then you came out of the hotel and you . . . kissed her.'

He picked up his brandy, swirled it around the glass and looked through its colour. 'What have I told you, Laura, about straying out on your own? You are a young woman of means now. You can no longer wander off at will. Your mother has no control over you and you show no desire to obey my word. What are we to do with you?'

'Father! Do not ignore me. I know you are having an af — a liaison with that woman. How could you?'

'Very easily. Do you think your mother cares? Do you think I care whether she knows or not? She has what she wants here — her house, her 'palace' — and I have what I want in

Mrs King, a warm-blooded woman who welcomes me and who smiles and laughs at my quips. And, Laura my dear, I will not give her up for anyone, not even you.

'But, my girl, for your own good you will be leaving us for a while and attending the Abbey School at Gorebeck, where a governess will instruct you in how to be a lady. For next year you will be married, and your errant ways will change. You have two possible suitors considering a match, and I will have you ready to meet whichever one I choose. You will act like a lady, and God help you if they find that you are a woman who scrambles around on her own, trespasses and disobeys her father's word. For a husband will not allow it, and I will not be able to come to your aid if you cross him. But marry, my dear, you will, for your own sake as much as ours.'

'I am too old for a governess to tutor me, and how can you think that Mother would not care about such a thing? If I saw you, our neighbours could, and the scandal would be terrible.' Laura was trying not to sob at the stark reality of her father's threat — a marriage was being arranged to a man who he was unaware had seen her pinned to a bank with her skirts awry. What a fool Daniel must think her. How lowly he would look upon her. He would never consider her suitable to be his wife.

'Laura, it is my hotel, and I have every right to go there when I wish to visit. I was careless this morning, but she had been afeard that I had perished in the storm, and I wanted to let her know that all was well.'

'I was worried, Mother was worried, so why did you not come to comfort us first? Don't we mean anything to you anymore?'

'Your mother would have been asleep; and you, my dear, you chose a different path. You have chosen to disrespect my commands and my wishes. I have therefore decided to find a man you will listen to, who is better placed to safeguard your future. Now leave me, and think on what I have said. You go to the Abbey School next week for two months of intense training.'

Laura wanted to strike out at him somehow. She did not like the way he had so selfishly dismissed her. 'Your boat is no longer in the stable.' She turned to leave.

'What?'

Laura had his attention now. 'I said — '

'I heard what you said, but what did you mean by it?' he asked, standing to his full height, his brandy forgotten.

'Just that. It is down with the other boats. Apparently Mother has a man coming about a carriage, and she wanted it out of the way.'

'Hell's bells!' He balled his fists and stormed past her and out of the house, making straight for the line of cobles on the beach.

10

Daniel set out to return to his mill. The eight miles were arduous, as the roads were heavy going. He thought about Miss Laura Pennington as he travelled. Whoever married that lady would certainly have an interesting life — or a troubled one. She was a natural beauty, but headstrong, although her tenderness toward Jeb showed that she had a warm heart. She was definitely her father's daughter.

However, her lack of judgement was a worry. Her naivety bordered on immaturity: to have gone onto the Hambletons' estate and leave herself so vulnerable was indeed foolish. But to marry such a woman? He expected to marry for love, not as part of a fiscal arrangement; but her father had made a good point. If he did not, then someone else would. Roderick had set his cap at the Hambleton wench, but she was spoilt and frivolous, and would tire of him within the first week of their marital bliss. No, Roderick would be sure to snap up Miss Pennington quickly after the rebuff from the Hambletons.

Daniel's mind calculated the chances and prospects of such a match, but what he returned to each time was that he would hate Roderick to get both the girl and the routes. First, he had his livelihood to protect: not only his own, but those of the whole community that relied upon the mill. Pennington knew the trade route well. He had contacts going back to a time when his trade was illegal contraband; now all of them flourished, and Daniel did not want to risk losing them. True, he could always start with other sailors and find new contacts, but that took time, and he trusted Obadiah — just as he also trusted him to keep his word and marry Laura off to someone else. Daniel had been his first choice — and that in the man's viewpoint was not an honour to be cast aside lightly.

His foreman, Simon Giles, met him with his usual friendly manner. Smiling, he took Daniel's reins as he stopped the horse by the dismounting block.

'There will be trouble here, Giles, if we do not act quickly to pre-empt it.'

The smile vanished from Giles's face.

'Call a meeting in the yard and bring me a box that I can stand upon. Place it so that they face me, and the mill behind. I want to speak to everyone: man, woman, girl or boy! And I want them to focus on what I am saying, and the livelihood that will be threatened if they do not support me. Arrange it as soon as is possible. Ring the bell when they are assembled, and I will come straight out.'

'Yes, Mr Tranton.'

* * *

An hour later, the bell sounded. Daniel walked out of his office and across the yard — directly through his workforce, deliberately emerging from the gathered crowd — and stepped proudly up on the box. He was already tall, but he wanted to be clearly seen to stress the message he was about to deliver. If he was to answer to anyone for the industry's treatment of its workers, then he would answer to them directly; for they toiled long hours to support his lifestyle, though few mill owners could see this. Instead, they saw the face of revolution in every reasonable request for fair pay or shorter hours for their children. Daniel did not; he saw one commonality: the look of desperation in their eyes and tiredness on their hungry faces.

'We cannot afford to stand around here, sir,' a solitary voice shouted out, but the noises of agreement revealed the mood of the workers. The message was true: troublemakers had been spreading ideas of dissatisfaction in the inn.

Daniel lifted both his hands to calm

the muttering and stirring that had begun, and then he raised his voice. 'Hear me out. Your wages will not be deducted for attending this meeting, or for the hour you will be given after it to talk amongst yourselves and decide upon your actions after hearing what I have to say.'

There was instant murmuring in the crowd. Curiosity was openly mixed with hostile suspicion.

'You have nearly all worked here since being children. Those who remember their first years' toil in the mill before I bought the place out will recall a very different environment to the one you now experience.' He looked around, deliberately seeking eye-to-eye contact with individuals that he knew, and was reassured as the older members of his workforce nodded and grunted their agreement.

'There is a rally one week from today. A meeting will be held up on Gorebeck Moor to discuss the rights and conditions of workers. It is supposed to discuss a fair wage and the number of hours of employment that may legally be expected for a child to work. It is supposed to address the complaints and issues that workers have with their employers. However, I have already given you my permission — the right to attend, not at your own expense, but on quarter-pay; whilst nearby mill owners have threatened sackings for those who attend, or no pay for the day. Am I being fair to you?' He shouted the question out and was relieved when all immediately nodded that he was.

'I have had a system of complaint set up here for two years, which has resulted in shorter shifts, warm soup suppers in winter, and better conditions for you and your children. Your food is provided freshly cooked, and is grown here on my land. It is shared fairly between the house and the workers. Is this not correct?' Again he bellowed out the question.

'Aye!' was the resounding response.

Again, his heart was filled with pride that these people whom he cared for in his own way were responding with gratitude for the concessions he had put in place. This had caused bitter resentment between him and his cousin.

'Therefore, I ask you this — do you still want to go to the meeting? Have you cause to go? And, if you do go, when the trouble breaks out because of interlopers from the west, hell-bent on breaking our machines — taking away your livelihood as well as mine — will you protect my mill, or let them destroy everything we have worked for together, to make your good living?'

There were gasps among some of the women, because such stark reality coming from his mouth had struck a chord. He normally spoke to them individually, but had few reasons to draw the crowd unless announcing a birth, a death or a marriage. Sometimes he felt like a priest looking after his flock, but it was a duty he took seriously. He noticed the downturned eyes of some of the younger men, and knew instantly that the rumours were definitely true: his mill had been singled out.

'I'd protect our mill!' shouted one of his older hands, a loyal man who knew when things were good; for he had lived through the bad times.

'And me!' 'And me!' The voices echoed from men and women and excited children who repeated the calls of their parents.

Daniel raised a hand to silence them all. 'Good. Then I ask another question: is there anyone here who would voice complaint and is still unhappy?'

Jerome Sleights stepped forward. 'You are a man who stands by his workers and his word, but your cousin is not. Ivor Bullman and his men run that mill as if it were their own. They make sure no complaint reaches the ears of their master, and he accepts that as his good running of it. Do you stand with him on this?'

'Jerome.' Daniel saw the man's eyes widen, as he had not expected him to know his name. But Daniel knew the name and family of everyone there. He made it his business to; they were as much a part of his enterprise, and essential to it, as the machines they controlled. 'I hear what you say; and if you all give me your word that you will set up shifts around the clock to protect our mill, then I will return to my cousin and try to dissuade him from any heavy-handed ways of dissuading his workers to attend the meeting.

'We are living in difficult times, but we have worked together here to grow our own food. I am looking at introducing new things. Not machines to take your jobs — though they will come — but essential trades so that this community can survive the harsh times by using the diversity of your labour. There is opportunity abounding if we work together, but we have to be flexible to get through the lean times. I give you my word that no one will be cast off, or starve on my land. But if these outsiders break what we have built up here, then the money I need to invest in new ventures will be taken by the need to mend broken tools. Then the future will not be so bright for any of us, and some might be laid off — though I would try to ensure that each family had one working member.'

Jerome shuffled his feet. 'It sounds like a threat wrapped up in promises,' he said, but others around him growled disapproval at him.

'My words are not threats; they are words of truth wrapped up in a shared vision of the future. If you have no wish to be a part of it, then you are at liberty to leave now, and spare these people the distress of having an outsider working against their interests from within our community.'

Jerome looked at the glares he was getting from his colleagues. The people he had grown up with and worked alongside were now doubting his loyalty. 'You speak the harsh truth of it. I'm a family man, and no outsider; and any man who makes such accusations against me again, no matter what his rank, I will ask to stand face to face with me like a real man and back them up.'

Daniel stepped down from his box, walked up to the strong figure of Jerome Sleights, and stared up at the man who was at least three inches taller than he. 'I will stand behind my words, and in front of you as a man, any time you care to call me out.'

Jerome, who had enough muscle to crush Daniel with one solitary balled fist, smiled back at him. The tense atmosphere dispersed instantly and Daniel felt his clenched innards relax slightly.

'You have my loyalty,' Jerome replied. 'Now show me your trust. Let me organise the shifts of men to protect the mill, whilst you sort Ivor Bullman out . . . sir,' he finished in a loud voice, and raised an eyebrow.

'Come to my office.' Daniel turned his back on the man and returned to his box. 'You all have until the bell goes in one hour's time to talk over what has been said. If you have no further questions or complaints, return to your shift, and no pay will be docked.'

The large figure of Sleights followed Daniel to his office. He stepped inside and Daniel wasted no more time. 'Close the door, Sleights, and explain your words,' he said as soon as they were inside the room. 'What did you mean by the comments you made about Bullman?'

'He oversees your cousin's mill.'

'I know what he does. And so?' Daniel wanted to hear what he suspected clarified by another who was better placed than he to discern the truth. He also wanted clear proof to show his stubborn-headed cousin.

'He makes it known that he dislikes the way you do things here,' Jerome continued, but Daniel felt that he was missing something more substantial, an unspoken something, more than repeated opinions.

'Be open, man. I will not hold anything you say against you, or spread it beyond these walls if you do not wish it known. I will give you my word that on this occasion, even if you incriminate yourself or Bullman in anything untoward, I will not seek punishment for you.'

'I'm not one of his henchmen. Very well, I'll tell you. He wants his men to control both mills so that they are run in the same way. If trouble is brought here, then your cousin will see that the liberties you allow us have gone to our heads. Therefore, he will insist on firmer controls being brought in here. Of course, he will seek Bullman's advice as to who should oversee them.'

'It is an interesting accusation, but you overlook one vital point: he has no right to do this, as this is my mill,' Daniel explained.

Jerome looked around the room. He was ill at ease, and Daniel was feeling a chill run through him.

'The only way he would gain control of this mill was if something were to happen to me,' Daniel added, and was taken aback when the other man looked him straight in the eye and raised an eyebrow, but said nothing further. The man could not hold his gaze for long, and glanced down.

'Are you suggesting that . . . ?'

'I've said too much already, sir, and much of it is speculation because I have no proof. But why would the word I have heard be directed at unsettling this mill rather than the one over Gorebeck way? There's been men, strangers, stirring up support for action in the local inns — tarring all your family with the same brush. But they've not been to the Hare and Hounds in Gorebeck — yet I saw Wilson, Bullman's right-hand man, in the White Hart last week, listening and chipping in his penny's worth, stirring up trouble right here in our own village.'

'It is a grand plan, but my cousin is not a man who could live with my blood on his hands. Think about the severity of what you imply.' Daniel was resigned to the possibility as he spoke, for in his heart he knew that Bullman and his comrades — all ex-soldiers

— could come up with any plan to remove him.

'With due respect, sir, your cousin rarely leaves his ledgers to inspect the mill, his stores, or the inn, where he would see Bullman acting like he was lord of the manor. He trusts the running and the discipline to Bullman. He would not suspect how far the man would go, for he is a gentleman of numbers — not a hard-nosed soldier raised in the gutter and carelessly returned there, left to make his own fate. If this mill can make profit, sir, with honest folk who work fewer hours for better pay than Gorebeck's mill, how is it then that their profits are less?'

'How would you know if they were or not?' Daniel was intrigued. This awkward giant of a man had revealed a situation that made perfect sense, even if it was uncomfortable to the ear.

Jerome clenched his lips tightly shut.

'You have gone too far already to stop. You may as well tell me all, and I swear no one who has not wronged me will be mentioned or punished. Beyond these walls, only I need to know the truth of it. So, whom do you protect?'

'I have been courting a lass from over there, who works in the house and helps in the office occasionally. She has a gift for numbers, and her writing is almost copperplate. He likes his ledgers real neat. She mentioned that the way things were, the mill was lucky to be still going. They cover their costs and your cousin's expenses, but not much more. Bullman sells and buys for Mr Roderick Tranton, but a cut is taken both ways. Small enough per bale not to be noticed, but over time like a year it makes a good supplement to his wages. This isn't written down, but when she told me how much he said he bought and sold for, I checked with me own cousin who knows the truth of it, for he is a merchant.'

'How long has this being going on?'

'A couple of years. It took Bullman a while to weave his way into a position of trust.'

'Thank you for your honesty.' Daniel thought for a moment. How could he get the proof he needed, and also his cousin's ear to take his claim seriously? If Sleights was not exaggerating, his own life could be at risk. 'Now answer one more question.' He took a deep breath before he formed the words he could barely believe he was asking. 'Would Bullman go so far as to arrange an attack on the mill as a smokescreen for the main intent — to murder me?'

Jerome looked him square in the eye, and gave his answer in one word: 'Yes.'

* * *

Laura had gone to her room, and remained there for most of the day. She had forgotten to mention Jeb; if the lad had been found, then his fate would be sealed. Her father had stormed out of the house like the devil was on his tail. She had never seen him so angry.

Laura had run past a shocked Annie, who had heard the door slam, and locked herself in her bedchamber. She had needed time to think. There was the elusive figure of Mr Daniel Tranton and the prospect of her father marrying her to him; yet this stranger must view her as a common wench. Besides, she was unsure if she could be made to marry if she did not wish to without disgracing her family or herself.

Then there was Jeb. What had become of him? And her father's declaration of love for the widow, Myrtle King — that was, if she had ever been ever married. Was it just a respectable title for his mistress to have and hold her head up high? If this was not enough, Laura had little time in which to plan or plead her case, for she was to be sent away to a school — at her age!

Hours passed, and still she had not made a decision on her next course of action. The more pressing the problems felt, the less able she was to make a decision. Her mother slept through it all in her laudanum-induced stupor.

Then there was a knock on the door.

'Who is it?' Laura asked.

'Annie. I have a tray for you.' Her voice was low.

'I'm not hungry.'

'There is a letter.'

Laura walked over to the door. Who would write to her now? And why? Her maudlin mood broken, she stood up, as this was too much of a mystery to leave unanswered. She opened the door. 'Please leave the tray on the table.'

Annie did so without question, but was looking at her. Once it was placed carefully down, she picked up the letter and handed it to Laura. 'What's happening, miss?' Her polite tone meant she was very curious and wanted to know what had gone so wrong with her day.

'Did you see the boat being taken away this morning?' Laura asked her while she stared at the envelope, her name penned in a strange but confident hand.

'Pa took it down to the bay with a

few of the men as Mrs Pennington ordered, but I only waved from the window as I wasn't up and dressed. So I did see them, but not to talk to.'

'Was there anyone there whom you did not recognise?' Laura asked.

'No, but why would there be?' Annie was standing next to her looking at the letter.

'No reason. It all seems a bit strange, the boat being moved without Father's knowledge.' Laura did not open it.

'Well, he was . . . busy,' Annie said, and smiled.

Laura stood straight and stared at her. 'Busy?'

'Are you going to open it, miss?' She ignored Laura's comment, which told Laura that at least one other person was well aware of his arrangement. And if she knew, did the whole of Ebton know of his affair as well?

'Yes, I will, after I've eaten.'

Annie was obviously disappointed. 'I thought you weren't hungry,' she said.

'Well, I am now.' Laura sat by the

table and poured out her hot chocolate from the china jug.

'I could help you if there's a problem, L . . . miss,' Annie offered.

'Thank you, I will let you know if there is.'

Annie left, slamming the door behind her.

11

Laura opened the letter and realised just how much of a problem she now had. It was from Mr Daniel Tranton and had been delivered by hand, but obviously not by his.

His apologies were heartfelt, or so they seemed. He begged her to ask for her father's help and to look after Jeb until he returned. He had the papers for his apprenticeship, so he was no longer being hunted and was quite safe. Daniel would return in a week's time after he had dealt with a pressing matter concerning his mill and the forthcoming worker's rally on Gorebeck Moor. Then, he added — and in these words the business-like tone of his message changed — they would be free to pursue more personal matters concerning her father's proposition and the way fate seemed to have crossed their paths and brought them together.

Laura stared at the letter. Fate? Was it true? Could a match between two people be as simply declared as that? Had 'fate' taken over her life? She was experiencing so much upheaval right now that she could only think fate might well have brought them together. But realising what a mess she was in, she knew it could also doom their relationship before it had even had a chance to begin and grow. Laura realised she now wished to have that chance.

She sighed. She had hidden a runaway who was no longer being pursued, but had managed to lose him. He had an injured arm, access to a pistol, and money, as well as a love and knowledge of boats. Her mind was reeling. He could set out on a life of crime in order to simply survive, as he had no idea that Daniel had kept his word. Jeb would not be able to handle a boat on his own, but could easily stow away.

Laura's father had always taught her

that when hunting an animal it was vital and respectful to make a quick kill, as an injured one was unpredictable and dangerous to pursue. Yet Jeb was not an animal, though he had been hunted. She laughed; her father had brought her up as a boy. She had gone out in the boats when young, fished and hunted — and on other men's land when needed; but now he was a respectable man of business. So she had been ordered to forget the hunger for adventure that ran in her veins. But how? What was she to do — change like him? She did not want to. She loved hunting and fishing — well, not the killing, unless it was to eat the prey. But she loved the thrill of riding in a boat on an unpredictable sea.

She leapt into action, her wallowing ended, and her day would begin again. She would seek out her father and ask for his help in finding Jeb; he could hardly lecture her about behaving badly, not now. However, first she must discover if the things hidden in the boat had been stolen from it. Or perhaps she should return to the woods to see if Jeb had gone back to the hiding place, waiting for Daniel to return to him.

* * *

Daniel set up a group of men armed with clubs who were to officially protect the mill should trouble arrive. These workers were his labourers — hard men who could plough fields and lift heavy goods, and whom he trusted. Sleights he had doubts about, but then he was not as familiar with him as the older men. But he needed someone younger and stronger to organise how they would regroup if needed, and to split them into shifts until the danger passed by.

Meanwhile, reluctantly, he had to return to see Roderick, after collecting the evidence to show the stubborn man that his overseer was a rogue: bills, to show him that his mill was being undermined by Bullman. He had to make the man swallow his pride and see sense. Daniel even thought about taking Sleights with him — but then that might show his hand to Bullman as he approached, before he was ready to. Preferably he would face him with soldiers to make an arrest for fraud and theft at the very least.

* * *

By the time Laura had made it down to the shoreline, the boat had gone — and so, it seemed, had her father, with Annie's father and some of the men. A few women sat clustered together mending nets and gutting fish.

She saw a woman she knew look up, but she did not respond to Laura's wave. It appeared there was some jealousy in the old town towards her family. Perhaps the cause was her mother's aloof attitude. Who knew? But Laura had to continue with her head held high as her father had taught her.

She walked up the muddy track

alongside the beck that ran along the gill and carefully placed her feet as it led her to the hiding place to seek Jeb; but her efforts were in vain, as there was no trace of him having been there since they left together. She remembered placing a bramble bush across its entrance to hide it further and that had not been disturbed. Unsure of why, and with little choice of an alternative action, she made her way back to town and straight for the hotel — their hotel, although she doubted her father would be back there so soon. But Mrs King might well know what he was about, whilst his wife slumbered on in her laudanum-induced sleep.

Laura took a few moments to straighten her skirts and to breathe three deep gulps of the fresh sea air. Now, more than at any time in her life, she wanted to appear as a woman in her own right. The door was answered by a maid.

'I wish to see Mrs King,' Laura announced. The girl knew her and so allowed her to enter the hotel, taking her into the reception.

'Good morning, Miss Pennington,' Mrs King's light-hearted voice greeted her as she entered the room. She was a tall woman who had a certain grace about her. Laura hated to admit it, but she was elegant. Her father had chosen a pretty mistress, not old enough to have faded looks, but not young enough to be flighty and restless with a good-humoured, mature man who obviously cared for her — or why else would he risk having her in charge of one of his businesses, and so near their home?

'My father — ' Laura began, but realised she did not really know what to say. She just wanted to face this woman who in the previous hours had become a husband-grabbing demon in her distraught mind.

'He is not here,' Mrs King answered, pre-empting the question.

'No, I thought not.' Laura stood, looking around her. She had only entered the building once, when it was purchased. Then it was plain and empty, but now it had been tastefully decorated. There was something striking about it; it felt loved in a way her home was not. The irony struck her hard, for this was a hotel; it was supposed to be impersonal, yet it was not — while her home lacked soul.

'Miss Pennington, are you not feeling well? Would you like something to drink? Perhaps you could join me in my parlour and we could talk there.' Mrs King stood aside and gestured that Laura should walk with her to the back room of the first floor. Laura did, not sure why, but she was now following her instincts. She had tried to rub as much mud from her boots as she could before entering, but next to this elegant woman she felt like a scullery maid, rather than a lady and the legitimate daughter of her lover.

This room was obviously Mrs King's own parlour. It had two chairs placed either side of the fire, which glowed with flickering warmth. Each winged chair was covered in pale blue chintz that matched the eyes of the lady who was watching Laura closely.

'Would it help if I said something to you first?' Mrs King offered, and Laura nodded without a word. She had come to this place in indignation, and as a brash act to confront the woman. Instead, she had been enveloped by a feeling she could not comprehend. It certainly was not hate. In fact, she could picture living in this place.

'I saw you this morning.' Mrs King sat before her, elegant and like Laura's own father had taught her, with a straight back and her hands folded gently in her lap.

Laura looked at her, but the woman was not being apologetic or defensive. Instead she gestured that Laura should sit by the fire. She then poured her a small brandy and offered it to her. Laura was about to decline, but the woman seemed to have a second sense. 'Take it, miss. Sip it slowly.'

'You saw me across the road. Then you know I saw you and my father . . . kissing,' Laura said quietly, and then sipped the brandy. It was good and warming and so she sipped it again. She blinked as if to see if this woman would vanish or change into a husband-stealing harpy before her eyes, but she did not. She was the same elegant female whom Laura had greeted at distance in their relatively brief encounters.

'You saw me say goodbye to Mr Pennington in a rash way that perhaps I should not have done. I apologise for that, but I will not apologise for loving a man whom my own father forbade me to marry.'

Laura's head shot up. What was she inferring? Her mind sifted through possibilities. Whyever would this genteel lady not be considered elegant enough for her rough-handed father? A tinge of guilt swept through her as she pictured her own sharp-eyed, fine-featured mother, who rarely had smiled even when Laura was a young child. One lady oozed quiet confidence and warmth, the other a detached air of self-absorption. It was not a loyal thought.

'He has not explained our story to you, has he?' Mrs King shook her head. 'Very well, I will, for otherwise you may resent me more than you already do.'

Laura could only blink at her and sip her lovely brandy. She had not eaten, and consequently its warming effect seemed all the more potent. She listened intently as the words washed over her.

'You father and I go way back. I was the daughter of the man who was the priest in the village church. I fell for the handsome rascal who was always trying to catch my eye from the back pews of the church when we left. He would come to the back of the vicarage and wait for me to appear in the garden and then surprise me. I loved him from the moment he first smiled at me.'

Mrs King broke off as she smiled at her private memories. Laura was transfixed.

'We became foolish and careless. A parishioner saw me laughing with him in the old town by his father's boat. My father was irate. He forbade me to see

Obadiah again. But Obadiah wanted to prove himself. Father never cared; he sent me away, and I was betrothed to Mr George King of Alunby, who lived at the other end of the bay. I had no choice; my alternative was to be sent to family, an aunt in Manchester.

'Your father, meanwhile, saved the village from burning with his quick thinking, and earned the gratitude of my father — but I was already wed. Your father took himself a wife, and well, that was the end of it, until my George went on the Gorebeck hunt and took a fall. He never recovered. He died two weeks later, and I was asked to leave our house, as he had accrued debts. He was a good man but did not know how to live within his means. George squandered his inheritance, and I had no idea that he had also used the money my father gave him as a marriage settlement.

'Obadiah heard about my situation when he saw the house was up for sale. Always one with an eye for a good deal, he bought it, realising I would be left homeless. He knew that my husband had been a hopeless dreamer who liked to spend and live a life that was too grand. He did not work, you see. Obadiah did it up and resold it, and with the profit he bought this place, and I moved in as the landlady.

'We never planned for our friendship to develop further, into an affair. It happened as if it was always was meant to be and I . . . I cannot say I have had any regrets, except that we cannot be together all of the time.' She smiled nervously at Laura. 'Neither of us wanted to break up your family. He would not do anything to hurt you.'

'But my mother, she is the victim here, lonely and — '

'Oh, please, do not be so naive, Miss Pennington. Your mother was a gold digger. She saw the success Obadiah could make of himself, and as soon as she could get him out of the old town she did just that, and in the process moved herself into her own rooms. He could not come into her house dirty — a man who risks his life on the high seas treated as hired help!' Mrs King flicked a glance at Laura's shoes, but smiled as she continued, 'Do you think she welcomes him to share her bed? They had one child, and you were not a son. Do you think he has had many chances to father another?' Her hand shot up to her mouth. 'I am so sorry, that was beneath me, cruel and crude. I apologise. I would never seek to hurt you. He loves you more than anyone in his life.'

'Except you,' Laura said boldly.

Mrs King coloured. 'You flatter me. But, Miss Laura, that is just not true. He would have you live a life away from the prison that your mother makes for you. She would have you docile and near. He loves you so much that he wants you to marry a man who will give you the life you desire — even if you do not know that yourself.'

'He would have me marry a man I do not know at all,' Laura corrected her.

The woman opposite her smiled knowingly. 'But that is not true, is it? You do know him, because you and the boy are waiting for him to return, are you not?' Mrs King smiled openly at her as once again Laura was lost for words.

'You know of Jeb?' Laura asked, but then cringed as she had said his name and admitted her part in hiding him.

'I found him curled up in my back yard earlier this morning when the men were moving the boat. Your father had left and I realised he was cold, hungry and scared.'

'Where is he?' Laura was frightened that he had been sent to the poorhouse. The more people who were involved, the more she would have let Daniel Tranton, and the boy, down.

'Fast asleep in my kitchen by a warm fire. He told me you helped him and that Mr Tranton will come back for him.'

'I have received word. Mr Tranton has his papers; Jeb is no longer hunted. He is now Daniel's apprentice. Can you tell him and keep him safely here, please? I need to find my father. I must speak with him.'

'Very well, I will put his mind at rest. His arm looks like it is healing well.'

'Thank you.' Laura stood up.

'Speak kindly to your father, miss. His only sin was to find true love when any form of love was denied him by his wife. He will never turn her out or divorce her. But she broke his heart; he stayed with her because of his love for you. But, let him be truly happy again.' She paused; and then, seemingly uncertain of whether to talk further, she spoke her mind. 'Should we be friends, Miss Pennington?' She stood and offered her hand.

Laura nodded. 'We should, because to be enemies would only cause Father greater pain. And neither of us wants that, do we?'

'No,' Mrs King replied.

Laura forced a polite smile. It would take time to trust these two people — her father especially, as she had held him so high in her mind.

She was led through to the kitchen, where Jeb was curled up in the chair fast asleep. Satisfied that he was indeed safe, she left.

12

Laura ran down to the old town. Her father was nowhere to be seen near his boats, so she broke another of his orders and went to the inn. She dared not enter the tap room, but skirted around the back. Old Amy occasionally sat on an upturned barrel mending nets, as it gave her something to do and reminded her of the old days. But instead of Amy, she saw her father talking to a grubby bearded man wearing a wide leather belt. She realised it was Alois Higgs, the gamekeeper.

'I tell you, Obadiah, the men are a-gathering, and there will be a trap set for him.'

Her father looked anxious. She had stopped at the edge of the inn and nestled behind a stack of three barrels. 'This cannot be. He is a good lad. Now, his cousin is a different kettle of fish

— him I can understand. He pays them a pittance and only gives them time to get over illness if they cannot stand. But Daniel . . . no, you must be mistaken. They have the wrong man and the wrong mill in their sights.'

'But that's just it — they ain't real machine wreckers. I worked over in the west for Hambleton. Believe me, he could make Mr Roderick Tranton look like a guardian angel. The man's family made money from slaving in the Indies, so they know how to work folk like dogs. But these men don't speak like they're from West Yorkshire; they're returners from the wars like Bullman and his cronies. There's only about five of them, but you don't need more than that to whip up a crowd. Panic and indignation spread as quickly as food would to hungry bellies.'

Obadiah shook his head. 'But Daniel's folk aren't starving.'

'That's not the reason they're a-watching him.'

'Well, you can tell your master that

his boat has been made ready and is on the beach waiting to go with his things still hidden safely within it. But the man is out of his mind. Why would they come for him here? What evil deed did he do that made him move across the land and expect to have to be taken over to Holland at a moment's notice? God's help will be needed if it is his own evil he runs from.' Obadiah was scratching his head.

'I think it is maybe only he who knows it, but these men that have arrived have nought to do with him. They are Ivor Bullman's, and they do not have Gorebeck Mill as the target of their venom, but Mr Daniel Tranton's.'

'Thank you, Higgs for telling me.' He looked up at the sky as Laura had seen him do so many times when seeking to catch an idea or for inspiration to come to him.

'Obadiah, word has it that they are not only planning to damage the mill, but to hurt him too. I don't know if this is to do with his wallet or him.'

'So what is in it for Bullman?' Obadiah asked.

'Control. He can twist Roderick Tranton around his little pinky because the man is scared of him and hides within his ledgers.'

'But to harm his cousin and take what is not his — ? If inheriting is what he seeks, it's nothing short of murder!'

'The cousin does not know how far the men he hires will go, but he will find out, and then he will be their puppet; for if he turns evidence on them, he incriminates himself. He is greedy and a fool, but not stupid enough to risk his own neck or profits.' Higgs raised an eyebrow and Obadiah had to see the sense in the man's words.

'Very well, I'll ride over tomorrow and warn him. We have time on our side if the meeting is not till Monday. This is a bad business, but keep it quiet. They'll be sorted out.' He entered the back of the inn, while Higgs made his way back up onto Hambleton's land.

Laura found it difficult to comprehend that Obadiah could think of drinking at a time like this. He should be doing something — warning Daniel now. If she heard correctly, he was in grave danger of being attacked and injured at the very least. There was evil approaching. Her father was most likely worn out by all his shenanigans, she thought uncharitably, so she would have to take matters into her own hands.

13

Laura went straight home and changed into her riding outfit. Her mother had insisted that she was taught how to ride, so that when they had the carriage to go regularly to the assembly rooms Laura would be able to quote riding as one of her accomplishments, along with her pleasant singing voice and fine needlepoint — when she had the patience to sit still and complete a piece. This, her mother hoped, would be enough to impress a suitor, along with her looks and dowry.

Laura had loved riding the most, experiencing the freedom of letting an animal take its head and gallop along the flat, sandy bay. She was as a free spirit trying to take flight. Her father had heartily disapproved. He said the beasts were untrustworthy, having fallen off one in his younger days. Laura's joy was short-lived, as Obadiah had the horse stabled at the hotel. It was frequently hired out to guests, and another attempt by her mother to move one step nearer owning two horses and a carriage had been thwarted.

When she was suitably attired, Laura went to the back of the hotel. The lad who tended the stable and saw to fetching and carrying for Mrs King was busy stacking logs in the barn.

'Saddle Misty for me,' Laura ordered. The poor lad dropped his burden, as she had deliberately wanted to sound authoritative and catch him off guard.

'Yes, miss . . . ' He hesitated after stacking the last log on top of the pile.

'Well?' she said, staring directly at him.

'Er, does Mrs King know that you're here? I mean, she didn't ask me to get him ready, and — '

'Do you know who I am?' she snapped, as he was wasting time, which was of the essence.

'No,' he answered honestly, and flinched when she answered.

'Miss Pennington. My father owns the horse, the stable and the hotel, and therefore pays your wages.'

He shot inside the stall and saddled the animal as quickly as he could, then emerged leading the horse out behind him.

'Thank you.' Laura quickly mounted the animal, tossed the chastened lad a coin, and rode off straight for the Gorebeck road. From there she could take the route to Daniel's mill. And, well, how difficult could it be to locate it?

* * *

Mrs King walked out of the back of the building just after midday. She saw the lad sweeping out the stable and looked around. 'Where is Misty?' she asked.

'Not back yet,' he answered as he diligently swept.

'Not back from where?' Her smile faltered as she asked the question.

'Miss Pennington hasn't come back

from her ride, miss. She said the horse was her pa's, so I thought . . . Have I done something wrong, Mrs King?' His big eyes stared hopefully at her.

'No, Ned, it is not you who has. Run down to the inn and see if Mr Pennington is there. If he is, ask him if he could come by, as Miss Pennington is still out on her ride.' She smiled to Ned as he ran off, now realising that indeed something was wrong, very wrong, because no one took 'the nag' out, as Obadiah called it, unless it was booked through her at the hotel. Whatever that girl was about, it was definitely without her father's knowledge. She only hoped that the naive young woman had not taken it into her head to run away. That would be disastrous for her reputation, and Obadiah would never forgive himself if he thought their love had caused the fall of his precious Laura.

Mrs King returned to her parlour and waited for the tornado of Obadiah Pennington to blow in. She would have to calm him down before he would be able to think straight and decide what to do.

* * *

Daniel was approaching Gorebeck when he saw three figures seated by the side of the road. One was standing, one was crouching, and the other was half-resting back on his elbows on the grass verge.

The one standing stepped into the road as he approached. His attire was different to the locals; he had a tall hat, a long grey jacket, and dark tweed trousers. He looked to Daniel like a troublemaker, so he kept his distance as he slowed the trotting horse to a standstill.

The man began to approach. He had his hands raised slightly, as if to show he meant no harm. 'Now then, mister. We come looking for work. You wouldn't know where we could find any, would you?' The man spoke clearly, with no hint of a local accent.

'You'd best try in town. What work

do you seek?' Daniel asked, but he now watched the two men who were sitting upright on the road's rough verge.

'Mill work — we are looking for work, like many in these parts and in the cities, but they don't hire anymore.'

'Then you'd best try the farms. There is usually work in the fields to do at this time.'

Daniel pulled at the reins to steer his horse to pass, when he noticed one of the men on the verge pulling something from his coat pocket. He sensed the change in the atmosphere. These men were seeking trouble; they could be part of the rabble brought in to target him and his mill. If so, he wondered if they had recognised him already. He had been a fool. Sleights had warned him and he had ridden out on his own, thinking that they would strike on Monday during the meeting. But why wait, if they could attack him now and be on their way?

His mind spun with decisions. Which one was the weaker? Could he bolt and make it into Gorebeck? A second passed that seemed like minutes, but then he heard pounding and realised it was not his head or his heart, but the noise of another horse's hooves thundering along the road, approaching from Gorebeck bridge.

Daniel sighed with relief as the men stood back and the man's hand returned into his pocket, but more than relief was his amazement to see Miss Pennington riding at speed toward him.

'Mr Tranton!' she shouted.

The men regrouped, discussed something briefly, then slipped away like shadows, making their way along a footpath that took them off down by the river, as Miss Pennington stopped her horse next to Daniel's. He automatically put out a hand to steady her as she pulled up quite quickly. Wisps of hair flew around her face, and he smiled. He was so happy to see her, full of life and energy as she was. She was so different to the pale faces he was introduced to at the side of their mothers when he was forced to socialise.

'I have never been so grateful to see anyone in my life before. But, Miss Pennington, we must enter town — and quickly. Please come with me, for we are not safe here.'

'Very well.' Without requesting an explanation, Laura did as he said. Despite her desire to inform him he was in some kind of danger, she rode with him into Gorebeck, where they quickly dismounted. He escorted her into the lounge of the Hare and Rabbit whilst a stable lad looked after their horses. Inside the dimly lit lounge, he led her to a corner table that was partially screened by a potted fern, and ordered a drink to calm both of them.

'Mr Tranton, you are in danger!' Laura blurted out as soon as they were on their own. 'Men are coming to hurt you in some way. They're not real, and . . . ' She pulled off her riding gloves and placed them on her lap. Her hands rested delicately on them.

Daniel leaned forward and gently

took hold of her hand, her fingers small against his. Laura did not pull hers away, but swallowed as she looked into his eyes, mesmerised by the intensity of his stare.

'How do you know this?' The concern on his face was touching as she watched his troubled brow crease. 'How are they not real?'

'Alois Higgs told my father they were coming for you. Father was going to leave it to come till the morning, but I decided that that would be too late, and so I tried to reach you today — only, we met on the road.' She smiled to try and break the tension she felt in his grip.

'Indeed we did, and it is just as well for you that you have no idea what you interrupted.'

'I do not understand, Mr Tranton.'

'You really have no idea, have you, my dear, sweet Laura?'

'Pardon?' she said as she felt his fingers relax.

He let go of her hand. 'I apologise. I behave badly.'

She instantly took his hand back in hers. 'No, not that. I mean, I like the sound of being your sweet . . . Well, I meant, what did I interrupt?'

He smiled at her as he gently and thoughtfully stroked her fingers, sending a wave of exciting sensations through her body that appeared to remove all her confusion and anxiety in one warm rush. This had been the most demanding of days; and yet, sitting opposite Daniel in their own little oasis of calm, it was rapidly becoming the best and most exciting one Laura had ever known. But he spoke to her in riddles.

'The three men, Laura — the ones at the side of the road where you found me. They were about to either ambush or hurt me. There was no one around and I unwittingly rode straight into them.' He shook his head as if he felt foolish in some way.

Laura swallowed again, only this time she looked at the man opposite — his handsome face, so strong; and yet his eyes so warm and, at that moment, vulnerable. She knew she could not bear to lose him before they had even had a chance to discover the joy of each other's company. Her father may have singled him out, but she would make her own choice. Right now she could think of no other person she would rather spend her time with and come to know.

'We should go to the militia!' she said. 'We must have them arrested.'

'But they have not done or said anything untoward, and I cannot have men arrested for merely thinking they may be about to do some evil deed. It is not enough to have them rounded up. No, Laura, unfortunately I need proof. And I know who is behind them — Mr Ivor Bullman.'

He let go of her hand as their drinks arrived. 'Where is Jeb?' he asked as he sipped the warm liquid from the china cup.

'He is in the safekeeping of Mrs King, who runs the hotel for Father.' She could not help it; her manner had changed, and her words were abrupt.

'Something troubles you about her?' he asked, leaning forward.

'She is nice enough, if you like . . . Never mind. What are we to do about those men?'

'You are not doing anything. I shall book you a room here — for you cannot return home today — and then I will see my cousin. I will have to decide what to do and if the militia should be involved or the magistrate.'

'My father will be very angry with me, I fear,' Laura admitted, but did not look at all guilty. 'I cannot stay here, as I have nothing with me.'

'My credit is good. I will have anything you need placed on my account.'

Laura laughed. 'No, that cannot be. Whatever would people say? I will just have to annoy Father further and place my purchases upon his account. May as well be hanged for a sheep as a lamb,' she said, and smiled.

'Why do I get the impression that you are not at all concerned whether your father is angry with you or not?' he asked.

'Perhaps because he . . . Well, let us say that if you preach morals and good behaviour, you should make sure that you set a good example yourself. He is usually a very honourable man, but his decision to delay coming to you was wrong.'

Daniel nodded. 'On that I would heartily agree.'

14

Obadiah stormed into the hotel and headed straight for the parlour. 'What has she done?' he demanded.

'Calm down, Obe,' said Mrs King. 'I don't know exactly what she has in mind, but she had no baggage with her and was apparently dressed in the appropriate attire for a ride. I have not seen her since she left here this morning when she went in search of you.' She watched as a look of surprise shot across Obadiah's face.

'She came here?' He looked incredulous. 'Did she hurl insult at you, or release a flurry of rage?' he asked.

'How little you know her, Obe,' she said, and noticed a tired, guilty spark in his eye.

'I've been busy. She was always such a headstrong child.'

'Yes, you nurtured and encouraged

that and now you expect her to sit in the parlour with her mama all day. I think not.' She stood and placed a comforting arm on his. 'Think, where would she have gone if she couldn't find you? What would make her take off so?'

Obadiah shrugged his shoulders and let out a long sigh. 'She came to look for me, you say? Well, I went to the inn. She wouldn't dare set foot inside it, or I would have her locked in an abbey for a month! No, there was no one by the boats; the only person I saw was . . . Oh, no, she could have been listening! The little fool.' He turned to storm back out.

'What is it, Obe?' Mrs King interrupted.

'Alois came to me at the back of the inn. He brought news of the trouble, trouble that could involve Daniel Tranton. But why would she act on that? She has no connection to the man yet.'

'Because they have met and they seem to like each other.'

'How?' he asked, and then as she looked to the kitchen, he nodded. 'The young lad, of course. Daniel was the one who helped him, yes?' Mrs King nodded. 'And that daughter of mine, always hanging out on the Hambletons' land, helped him somehow, didn't she?' She nodded again.

'By all that's sacred, I swear I will sort that lass out. She will be wed before winter comes, if her reputation does not already lie in ruins. I'll have to take a nag from the inn and ride over the moor road. Damn! If it's the death of me, you tell her — '

'Obadiah Pennington, what grim message would you have me impart to a grieving daughter who loves you deeply and has been shocked to the core to learn that you love another woman in a very different but equally deep way?'

'Tell her that next to you she is the only woman I have ever admired and loved. But I will return safe. No stupid animal, other than the one I married, will ever get the better of me.' He stormed out, but Mrs King could not help but laugh at him and his ways, even if the joke was on them, because he was married — and that meant, as Mrs Pennington knew so well, they could never be whilst she breathed.

* * *

Daniel knew that Roderick would have left the mill by now, so instead of seeking him in his office, he headed straight for the house he owned, which was in a separate part of town. The man had sense; he had no wish to breathe in his own manufactories' fumes.

Roderick was just finishing his dinner when Daniel walked in, ignoring a protesting house maid. 'You, again!' He swallowed the last of his glass of wine as if Daniel were going to rip it from his hands. 'Do you always have to burst in as though the devil himself were after you?'

Daniel closed the door behind him as Roderick waved the maid away.

'Out with it, then. What brings you here this time?'

Daniel walked up to the end of the long table and stood to the side of his cousin whilst keeping an eye focused through the window on the main road into Gorebeck over the bridge. 'You must listen to me, Roderick, and take my words seriously,' he began. He noticed a rider in the distance, approaching the town at a pace.

'But you say nothing.' Roderick coughed. 'Port?'

'No, it's about Bullman. I tell you, he is a bad egg, and he is trying to do us both harm. I have proof that he is cheating you and seeks to run both the mills with his own men.' Daniel glanced at the man who seemed unperturbed about his revelation. 'He would do us harm, man!'

'Must I listen?' Roderick sat back in his chair and looked up at Daniel, who was realising that the rider was Mr Obadiah Pennington.

'Yes!'

'So what do you want me to do? Sack him or have him arrested as a swindler, or wait until he strikes and have him hanged for hiring men to take you down?' He raised one brow.

Daniel's head spun around as he saw the smug expression on Roderick's face. 'You knew?'

'Ah, you think me so stupid. Who is it that spends his time looking at ledgers to make sense of the numbers? Who is it that has seen his profits dwindle in the last year? Me! That's who. You do not know everything about me, my young cousin.'

'You know about his men, the ones he brought in to do me harm, and you never said a word? Are you in on this, Roderick?' Daniel clenched his fists at his side to stifle the overwhelming emotions that tore at his heart. He had never been close to Roderick; admittedly he had enjoyed bettering him in sport, cards and with the fairer sex, but he had never thought that the man would partake in his downfall.

'No, Daniel. I would not break the law and risk everything my father worked for just to spite you. My father-in-law-to-be, Hambleton — ' He smiled as he paused to see Daniel's curious expression. ' — knew Bullman from before the wars. He recognised him on a trip to town and left straight away before the man could see him. The following day I was asked to visit him privately. He told me that Bullman was a hardened soldier who had taken the king's shilling to avoid a life in gaol. He had been a troublemaker, but it was Hambleton who had him arrested back then, and the man swore he would seek his revenge if ever they crossed paths again.'

'So what is all this to do with me?' Daniel asked, intrigued by this change in Roderick's confident manner.

'Nothing. I have been working with Captain Gillick at the barracks. We have given the man enough slack to hang himself, and can put his ruffians away for good. He wants the three who were loitering on the road for you. You see, you have been watched.'

Daniel saw an irate Obadiah Pennington dismount outside the house. 'Not always,' he said.

'Oh, yes, for who else but a man with local knowledge could send a hunt in the wrong direction, instead of leading him straight to a fool who should not be muddying his boots to save an urchin like Jeb?' Roderick heard the loud knock on the door and shouted to the maid, 'Let him in.'

The door opened and Pennington blustered in. He stared at Daniel and then looked to Roderick. 'My daughter, she . . . '

'Your daughter is at the hotel, safe,' Daniel answered.

'She heard the groundsman talking to me about Bullman's heavies. She can't have realised that I was waiting for the militia to take their places.'

'Why did you not tell me? Either of you?' Daniel asked.

Roderick stood up and laughed. Daniel could not remember when he had seen him look so genuinely animated and happy. 'For the simple reason you would have changed your behaviour. Tried to outsmart them, as you always try to do me, but not this time. I have the militia about to descend on the Hare and Rabbit, where they are all meeting in the tap-room. They will be rounded up. I'll have my money back in my bank, and I'll announce my marriage to the beautiful Miss Sarah Hambleton in the coming month, as her father is so very grateful to me for removing the shadow that has been cast over his life since that fateful day when he saw Bullman. So, gentlemen, if you will excuse me, I will bid you good day, the maid will show you out.' Roderick strode purposefully out of the room.

Obadiah looked at Daniel. 'Sorry, lad,' he said, but Daniel smiled back at him.

'Don't be, sir.'

'Do you not feel put out?' Obadiah asked.

'No, let him have his moment of pride. I've had my share over the years, but he will regret the day he married that empty-headed, fickle girl. She'll cost him a fortune, and her father is as strong as an ox; he'll no doubt outlive Roderick, and he is tight. No, Roderick will suffer, just as his wallet will.

'I'd better see my daughter. We have things to settle.'

Daniel nodded. 'May I come? I would like to make good on your offer if she is open to it.'

Obadiah sighed. 'She is angry with me. She knows about Mrs King, Daniel, and is a girl still; she will not understand.'

The maid opened the door. 'I think you underestimate her,' Daniel said as they left the house.

Obadiah looked shocked. 'That is the second time today I have been told I do not know my own girl!'

'Then that is the heart of it, for she is a girl no longer,' Daniel remarked, and made his way directly to the hotel.

* * *

The commotion at the inn caused the whole of the population of Gorebeck to stare out of their windows as Ivor Bullman and his men were arrested. They were given a choice on the spot of marching off with the King's shilling in their pocket, or going to gaol until their cases could be heard in York assizes. Most marched.

Laura watched the men, but not the soldiers; it was her father and Mr Tranton — Daniel — who walked toward the hotel. She decided to take a seat at the side of the small lounge and await their arrival rather than be found staring out at the spectacle. Besides, if she was in a public area of the hotel, her father was less likely to explode at her most recent adventure and proof of her total lack of respect of his wishes to refrain from riding, venturing out on her own and generally disobeying his instructions. She could see her future ensconced within an abbey wall of the finishing school as a certainty.

They entered. Laura swallowed as

they walked over to her, pulling two chairs with them so they could sit by her.

'Laura . . . '

'Father. Mr Tranton.' She smiled and looked from one to the other. Her cheeks felt warm and she hoped she had not coloured too deeply.

'Laura,' her father continued, 'what am I to do with you? I have built a small fortune to settle on your future — my legacy to you and your children, when you have them — and yet you are still so reckless,' he said in a calm manner.

'Well, I thought . . . ' She looked at Daniel, who seemed to be almost biting his lip to hold back his words until her father had spoken his first.

'Yes, you thought. You did not ask me, child.'

'I tried, but you were otherwise engaged.' She tried not to provoke his anger further, but looked at him directly. To her surprise, he spoke to Daniel.

'I have let the girl down, and now she

is a wilful woman. Do you think you can become engaged to such a woman and make a good marriage?'

Daniel smiled, but Laura snapped, 'I will not be discussed in such a manner as if I am not here, Father. I may have acted rashly, but in a good cause. You were going to leave Daniel, and men were trying to hurt him. I saved him from them!'

'Did she?' Obadiah asked.

'Yes, in a way she did. I may have been watched by Roderick's soldiers, but there was a very strong chance they could have acted before they could have been stopped. It would appear that fate has brought Laura and me together. If it is with the approval of both of you, I would like to walk out with her.' He paused, turning to Laura. 'I would like to consider an engagement between us. It seems both of us have a tendency to act rashly; and I think if I have learned nothing else, it is that perhaps I cannot do everything in life on my own.'

Obadiah stood. 'Laura, you have my

blessing to be with this man and to consider your future. I shall arrange rooms here tonight for us both and a carriage to take us home tomorrow. You can let me know your decision then. But you will need to learn to behave properly, and — '

'No threats, Father. I will not let you down. I am too old for school, but it seems I still have a lot to learn.'

Obadiah nodded and walked away.

'Mr Tranton . . . '

'Daniel, please.' He smiled.

'Daniel, I would like us to become better acquainted. Could I come and stay near your mill if Mother would chaperone me, so I can know the man you are and the life you live?'

'Yes. Would you share my dreams of a future where a community cares for its workers?'

'Yes,' she said excitedly, and held his hand, forgetting where they were, but happy to have found a soulmate with whom she could share her life.

Books by Valerie Holmes
in the Linford Romance Library:

THE MASTER OF
MONKTON MANOR
THE KINDLY LIGHT
HANNAH OF HARPHAM HALL
PHOEBE'S CHALLENGE
BETRAYAL OF INNOCENCE
AMELIA'S KNIGHT
OBERON'S CHILD
REBECCA'S REVENGE
THE CAPTAIN'S CREEK
MISS GEORGINA'S CURE
CALEB'S FAITH
THE SEABRIGHT SHADOWS
A STRANGER'S LOVE
HEART AND SOUL
BETHANY'S JUSTICE
FELICITY MOON
THE VALIANT FOOL
TABITHA'S TRIALS
THE BAKER'S APPRENTICE
RUTH'S REALITY
LEAP OF FAITH
MOVING ON

MOLLY'S SECRET
CHLOE'S FRIEND
A PHOENIX RISES
ABIGAIL MOOR:
THE DARKEST DAWN
DISCOVERING ELLIE
TRUTH, LOVE AND LIES
SOPHIE'S DREAM
TERESA'S TREASURE
ROSES ARE DEAD
AUGUSTA'S CHARM
A STOLEN HEART
REGAN'S FALL

We do hope that you have enjoyed reading this large print book.

Did you know that all of our titles are available for purchase?

We publish a wide range of high quality large print books including:
Romances, Mysteries, Classics
General Fiction
Non Fiction and Westerns

Special interest titles available in large print are:
The Little Oxford Dictionary
Music Book, Song Book
Hymn Book, Service Book

Also available from us courtesy of Oxford University Press:
Young Readers' Dictionary
(large print edition)
Young Readers' Thesaurus
(large print edition)

For further information or a free brochure, please contact us at:

Other titles in the
Linford Romance Library:

STORM CHASER

Paula Williams

When Caitlin Mulryan graduates from university and returns to Stargate, the small Dorset village where she grew up, she is dismayed to find that the longstanding feud between her family and the Kingtons is as fierce as ever. Soon her twin brother is hunted down in his boat *Storm Chaser* by his bitter enemy, with tragedy in their wake — and Caitlin can only blame herself for her foolish actions. So falling in love with handsome Yorkshireman Nick Thorne is the last thing on her mind . . .

THE PARADISE ROOM

Sheila Spencer-Smith

The stone hut on the cliffs holds special memories for Nicole, who once spent so many happy hours within its walls — so when she has the chance to purchase it, she is ecstatic. Then the past catches up with her when Connor, the itinerant artist she fell in love with all those years ago, reappears in her life. But has his success changed him? And what of Daniel, the charismatic sculptor she has recently met? Nicole's heart finds itself torn between past and present . . .